Love in Lutyens' Delhi

Amitabh Pandey studied Economics at St Stephen's College and Delhi School of Economics. He taught at an undergraduate college of Delhi University and then joined the Indian Railways where he worked for twenty-four years, during the course of which he conceptualized, implemented and managed the Railways' online ticket reservation system at the IRCTC. In 2007, Amitabh shifted to the private sector and spent five years building business software. He now lives in Noida and writes full-time.

Love in Lutyens' Delhi

AMITABH PANDEY

For Navoshi & Madhavan

Enjoy!

Amit
Jan '18

PAN

First published in India 2017 by Pan
an imprint of Pan Macmillan Publishing India Private Limited
707, Kailash Building
26 K. G. Marg, New Delhi - 110001
www.panmacmillan.co.in

Pan Macmillan, 20 New Wharf Road, London N1 9RR
Basingstoke and Oxford
Associated companies throughout the world
www.panmacmillan.com

ISBN 978-93-86215-22-2

Copyright © Amitabh Pandey 2017

This is a work of fiction. All characters, locations and events are fictitious.
Any resemblance to actual events or locales or persons, living
or dead, is entirely coincidental.

All rights reserved. No part of this publication may be reproduced, stored
in or introduced into a retrieval system, or transmitted, in any form, or by
any means (electronic, mechanical, photocopying, recording or otherwise)
without the prior written permission of the publisher. Any person who does
any unauthorized act in relation to this publication may be liable to
criminal prosecution and civil claims for damages.

1 3 5 7 9 8 6 4 2

This book is sold subject to the condition that it shall not, by way of trade
or otherwise, be lent, re-sold, hired out, or otherwise circulated without
the publisher's prior consent in any form of binding or cover other than
that in which it is published and without a similar condition including this
condition being imposed on the subsequent purchaser.

Typeset by SÜRYA, New Delhi

Printed and bound in India by
Replika Press Pvt. Ltd.

For Sandhya

Prologue

NOBODY NEEDS AN INTRODUCTION TO LOVE BUT MANY may not be familiar with the salubrious city of Delhi, hence this Prologue.

Delhi is, quintessentially, about power and all that flows from it. The centre of power in the city is located geographically to the south in an area often referred to as Lutyens' Delhi after Sir Edwin Landseer Lutyens (1869–1944), the architect who designed, amongst other things, the grand monument to colonial power now known as Rashtrapati Bhavan.

Lutyens' Delhi, in our context, refers to the senior sarkari portion of New Delhi where power, and those who wield it, reside. In the chaotic, crowded, noisy and polluted city of Delhi it is a green and gracious oasis of bungalows with manicured lawns, parks with huge old hardwood trees – and classical music concerts in good weather – wide, clean roads gleaming with black tar and white paint and bored chauffeurs leaning out of windows of the now swanky government cars. Also, there are no power cuts or water shortages. Some even say the summer sun shines more gently here than elsewhere and the moonlight is cooler and more beautiful. Be that as it may, it's a very nice place to live in.

Along the edges of the zone the bungalows fade away and blocks of flats appear for those not quite so senior, but important nonetheless; you don't live here if you're not important. As the Jedi Master said, 'There's always a bigger fish,' and, besides, what would be the meaning of life if one couldn't move from a DI-type flat via a CII to a bungalow on Tughlak or Akbar Road.

Beyond the pale, to the south, lie the private colonies of the well-to-do – Green Park, Hauz Khas, Shantiniketan et al – and then you hit the wilds of what used to be called Gurgaon.

A poet once insisted that 'when love is waiting, logic will not do …' But the more cynical amongst those familiar with Lutyens' Delhi maintain that when a plum posting is waiting love is not enough.

The less cynical, however, claim that love will always, somehow, find a way.

1

'ALL RIGHT, LITTLE BEN OF MINE, OUT WITH IT,' SAID Gayatri, draining her glass and putting it down with a snap on the side table. 'I've been waiting for three months for you to come clean and now even young Akku, who is growing up rather fast in case you hadn't noticed, is asking what's happened to her beloved Abha Maasi. So, time to tell all – what is it? Or rather, who is it?'

It was a cold winter evening in Delhi and Gayatri and Abha had been sitting by the heater in the living room in companionable silence. Akriti, Gayatri's daughter, in the final year of her BTech programme, had left for her hostel and the sisters had opened a bottle of wine to keep the chill at bay.

The two presented a striking picture as they sat together in the living room of their large rented flat in New Delhi's Hauz Khas. Both had large brown eyes and thick, unruly black hair cut short, but there the similarities ended. Gayatri was slim, tall and fair like her mother, very pretty in a subdued, quiet sort of way. Abha, on the other hand, was short and dark like her father, and dazzling – vivaciously attractive with a smile and dimples that could, as a literate admirer once said, induce even a man of the cloth to 'kick a hole in a stained glass window'. She was a senior commissioning editor at one of the biggest multinational publishing houses to set up shop in India.

'What on earth are you talking about?' she asked her sister, eyebrows raised. 'And, for the middle of the week, you are drinking a little too much, doctor saab!'

Gayatri smiled. 'Don't be clever with me, li'l sis – diversions won't work. Something has changed for the better and I want to know what, but only after you pour me my second small glass of wine of the evening, and yourself your third!'

Abha picked up the glasses, filled them up to the brim and came to sit next to her sister.

'Nothing gets past you, does it? Okay, I've met someone I like very much, but as always it's a messy situation and I don't know where it will end up. So, that's it.'

'Oh no, it isn't,' said Gayatri. 'Not one of your temps, I take it. So what's the mess? I'm an expert at sorting out messes, in case you don't remember.'

Abha smiled.

'Well, he's mine, he's married and he's Muslim. How's that for a difficult situation, big ben?'

'Then we'll get him a talaq, have a court wedding and a big reception – where's the problem?'

Abha then did something she hadn't done since she was a little girl. She put her head in her hands and wept, silently and for a long time.

Gayatri put her arm around her sister's shoulders and held her gently.

When Abha was done, she went to her room, washed her face, came back and poured a large whiskey for herself and what remained of the wine for her sister.

'I swore I was done crying over men, but obviously I was wrong,' she said, anger and a touch of despair in her voice.

'Insulations wear off, my dear,' said Gayatri gently. 'And that's good, because then you can start feeling again. No fun otherwise. So, why can't he get a divorce and marry you?'

'Because she won't give him one, even though they've been separated for ten years now. Theirs was a college romance – she's an Ismaili – and they had a court wedding. And then, after eight years and two kids, they drifted apart irreconcilably. She's a successful businesswoman in Mumbai, while he's a senior political journalist in Delhi. You see, he has family money – lots of it.'

'Ah, that explains a lot. Where was college?'

'LSE. He studied Political Science, she Economics.'

'Good for them. So what do you intend to do? Set up house with him?'

'At this point, no. Things are fine as they are. This remains my home – with your permission, ben – until we are clearer about everything. But yes, for now I do wonder by my troth what he and I did till we loved! By the way, what exactly did your little minx of a daughter say?'

'Almost exactly what I've been asking! "Abha Maasi looks very happy these days –what's happened?"'

Abha laughed.

'Growing up too bloody quickly, isn't she? Just the other day that I took her to school for her first kindergarten class. Remember, you had an emergency at the hospital?'

'Couldn't forget if I tried, li'l ben. You've been as much mother to her as I have, if not more, Abha. But

I'm now concerned about her thing with Sanju. Where is it headed?'

'I don't know, ben, but at this stage all we can do is keep a careful watch and give it time. They're still so young.'

2

THE WINTER SUN POURED IN THROUGH THE WINDOW, filling the rather unprepossessing room with light and warmth. Akriti and Sanjay lay cosily entwined beneath a quilt on a mattress on the floor.

'Remember our first day at school? You came all weepy and untidy and sniffled and snuffled all morning till I gave you all the goodies Maasi had packed for me. All I got were your soggy stale sandwiches and even soggier chips!' said Akriti.

'All I remember is that I was miserable. Papa was in New York and Mummy had to rush for some super urgent meeting so Papa's driver took me to school. But it was sixteen years ago, stupid! You can't possibly remember what we ate or wore or said – you're just fantasizing,' replied Sanjay.

'Fantasizing my arse!'

'Hmm, yes,' he said reaching out and squeezing the said portion of her anatomy. They had just had some very vigorous, mutually satisfactory, though not especially skilful sex and were in post-coital mode – she cheerful and chatty, he weary and inclined to doze off.

'Get your hands off, and listen. But if you want to sleep, I'll just get back to my hostel.'

That woke him up, as she knew it would. He pulled her to him and said, 'I'm listening, baba. I listen best with my eyes closed, is all.'

'You piggo!' She giggled, cuddled up and continued to reminiscence. 'I remember everything, Sanju baba, from about the age of three, I think. Especially everything to do with you!'

They met for the very first time in kindergarten at age four. She arrived ten minutes early, hopping with excitement, face freshly scrubbed, hair organized into two tight plaits held together with pink ribbons, shoes shining, snack box and water bottle neatly packed in a bright red and blue schoolbag!

'Go away now, Maasi,' she said impatiently to the young woman who had driven her to school. 'I'll be okay now. Go, bye.'

As little Akriti skipped into school, the teacher on gate duty smiled at Maasi aka Abha Patel.

'Very few children are so happy on their first day at school. You are very lucky, ma'am. Most of them are like that young man over there.'

The little gentleman in question had emerged from a chauffeur-driven sarkari Ambassador, tear stains on his cheeks, snot on his upper lip and a thoroughly miserable, woebegone expression on his face. The chauffeur took a firm grip on this reluctant student's arm, led him to the gate, ushered him in and left.

'Come, Sanjay, let me take you in,' said the on-duty teacher and escorted her unhappy charge inside. Abha left, smiling to herself.

'Remember the first time you tried to act funny in the movie hall in class ten? I was so upset I wrote to Maasi; she was in Almora with her boyfriend at the time.'

He sat up with a start. 'You told her about it? What the hell for? No wonder she hates my guts! You are a stupid ninny, Akku – there are some things you just don't talk about!'

'So you're worried Abha Maasi will land up with a shotgun if she learns we're screwing, huh? What a scared little mouse you are, lover boy! And she doesn't hate you at all. But speaking of mice, where is my favourite little rodent? Fast asleep, just as I thought. Well, I'd better wake him up to some action, because I have to leave soon. Come on, little rodent,' she said groping beneath the quilt. 'Wakey, wakey, you have work to do.'

'You'd better do some work first,' he replied hoarsely, pushing her head down.

'Don't push, idiot! I'm coming, little mousey, I'm coming.'

The assignation was in his hostel room in the red-brick Mission College on Delhi University's north campus. He was in the final year of his English Honours course, while she was studying Computer Science across town at the Indian Institute of Technology. It was Sunday and she had come down because there was no way he could get into the girls' hostel in her institute, whereas sneaking into his hostel was not particularly difficult. When she insisted she absolutely had to leave, he walked her to the bus stop. He never offered to escort her back to Hauz Khas and she never asked.

Akriti changed buses at Central Secretariat. As the ancient vehicle ground through Lutyens' Delhi, she recalled Abha Maasi's reply to her frantic letter after Sanju's first clumsy attempt at making a pass in a movie hall. He started off smartly enough, reaching for her hand that had been lying conveniently close to his for quite some time on the shared armrest. Then, encouraged by her silent approval, he mustered up courage and ventured northwards. There was some awkward fumbling, but soon he reached his goal – and ... Akku almost screamed. She yanked off his hand, jabbed him with her elbow and managed to keep her voice down to a muffled, indignant squeal. Someone in the row behind giggled and the rest of the movie was spent in silence and with as much distance as can be maintained between two people sitting together in a cinema hall. Complete silence reigned on the journey home as well. Seeing her off at her door, Sanju managed a gruff and barely audible 'Sorry' before turning and stomping away.

Akku was furious. She was quite prepared to accept a sincere and lengthy apology, and here the fellow just muttered something lame and marched away. She slammed the door, ran up to her room and dashed off a letter to Abha Maasi. The reply came by return mail a week later.

My dear Akku,

So my little girl is growing up, huh? Messing about in cinema halls and then getting scared and pushing away! Don't worry, darling, absolutely normal as long as that idiot friend of yours did not persist, as I gather he didn't. The two of you will soon be adults and transitions are terribly uncomfortable – all the fear and uncertainty! Happens to everyone, so don't worry, just take it slow and easy. Don't be rushed into anything that you don't feel ready for. Remember, men can be pushy about the whole sex thing; but be firm, don't get coerced. For now, just relax and forgive him, when you think you're ready. Use whatever buddhi you have – that's the best you can do at any point in time. I'll be in Delhi in two weeks so we'll talk then.

Take care of yourself, and lots of love to your mother.

Abha

3

SOON AFTER SHE STARTED SCHOOL, AKKU RAISED a question her Abha Maasi had been expecting and dreading for a while. The bedtime story had been read, the goodnight hug exchanged and the bedside light switched off, when suddenly Akku said, 'Maasi, everyone in school has a pappa except me. How come I don't have one? They all laugh at me when I say I don't.'

It was Friday night and twenty-five-year-old London-educated Abha Patel, editor and swinging single, was planning a night on the town after putting her little niece to bed. The question, however, put paid to the party mood in an instant. She took a deep breath and sat down next to Akku.

'Of course you have a pappa, Akku, only he doesn't live with us any more.'

'But why?'

'Because he died some years ago, baby. He fell very ill all of a sudden and died.'

'But Mummy is a very good doctor, no? Why didn't she make him well?'

'Sometimes even the best doctors cannot do that, child.'

'But that's not fair. No one else's pappa has died.'

'Everybody's pappa will die some day, Akku. Some sooner than others. That's how life works.'

'But it's not fair, Maasi.'

'That's the way it is, baby. We just have to carry on as best we can.'

'I don't care what you say; it's not fair. I wish I had my pappa like everyone else.' Akku turned away, buried her head in her pillow and quietly cried herself to sleep, while Abha sat by her side patting her gently and staring into the darkness.

When Akku was asleep, Abha went to her sister who had returned from the hospital a while ago and was settling down with a book in the living room.

'You're running late for your date,' remarked Gayatri, looking up from her book.

'Akku just asked me why she does not have a pappa like everyone else in school.'

'And what did you say?'

'The simple truth – that he fell very ill suddenly and died.'

'And her response?'

'It's not fair.'

Gayatri put down her book and sat back in her armchair.

'She's learning that rather early, poor little thing.'

'Yes, she is, and it breaks my heart, ben, but that's the way it was going to be.'

'Indeed,' Gayatri sighed. 'Well, hurry up, get ready and go. Don't keep him waiting, whoever it is tonight.'

'No rush, and anyway they have to learn some patience if they want to deal with me! Besides, I have an idea – why don't you come along? There are always many nice singles hanging around the bar we're planning to hit; I'm sure you'll meet someone interesting. C'mon, ben, it's time you got out a little.'

Gayatri smiled in genuine amusement.

'I'm not twenty-five any more, Abha. I need my rest over the weekend to keep up with my surgery schedule during the week. And I'm not ready to look at men that way yet, not sure if I ever will be, but that's beside the point. Go on, before he gets tired and moves on to someone else.'

'Someone else? Wait till you see what I'll be wearing, big ben,' Abha said and marched off to her room.

Gayatri kept quiet with great effort – it was never wise to try and dictate propriety to her sister; you never knew what her reaction would be, the mad girl. But to be fair to her, she was very savvy about the world, always knew what she could get away with, where and with whom, thank God!

Half an hour later, the vision that walked into the room made Gayatri exclaim in shock. 'Do up some of the buttons, girl. Can't have everything hanging out like that!'

'For heaven's sake, big ben, I'm a woman, I have boobs! And on occasion, I flaunt them a little. What's the big deal? And just by the way, you should see what the teens are wearing these days!'

'Nothing much, I presume. Silly girls. They don't realize that the mystery is the most important thing.'

Abha laughed and patted her sister's shoulder.

'The mystery, my dear, lies in the flavour of the condom he's carrying. Times have changed, darling ben; I wish you would keep up!'

'Shoo now, go away. And, Abha, don't drink too much, okay?'

'Sure, but I'm not driving, so we'll see. Don't wait up.'

Abha left in a cloud of Anais Anais and Gayatri returned to her book. Five minutes later she put the book down, took out a bottle of white wine from the fridge and poured herself a glass.

'No self-pity now, no tears, no why me. You feel like a drink, have one,' she told herself sternly. She sat in her favourite armchair, a small lamp switched on beside her, sipped her wine and read late into the night.

When Abha returned in the early hours of the morning, she found her sister in the armchair fast asleep, book on the floor and the bottle of wine empty on the table.

'For Christ's sake, ben,' she muttered to herself as she woke Gayatri up and watched her walk slowly to her bedroom. 'When will you fucking stop grieving and start living again?'

She got no answer of course, so she went to bed and slept till lunchtime. It had been a long night.

4

WITHIN A FEW YEARS OF STARTING SCHOOL, IT WAS evident that both Akku and Sanju were very bright children, gifted almost, but in markedly different ways. Akku was good at most subjects, but way ahead of her class in logical reasoning and mathematical understanding, while Sanju was remarkably proficient in the English language. He read much beyond his age group, had learnt to use the dictionary early and was rapidly building up a strong vocabulary. Mathematics, however, was a serious struggle.

'God, you are a dumbo, Sanju,' exclaimed Akku when trying to initiate him into the mysteries of the decimal system before one final exam. 'Better stop reading all those silly adventure novels and focus on the numbers or you're going to almost fail again and your mom will be furious.'

The threat had immediate effect – Sanju sat up and concentrated on the matter at hand. Both nature and nurture had combined to instil in him an overpowering need to come first always and in everything– ambition was one value both his parents had made him internalize comprehensively.

For Mrs Rashmi and Mr Rajiv Saran, the meaning and purpose of existence was to be number one. Having completed their field postings with distinction, this meant Central Government deputations in 'good' ministries. Mr Saran, the Economics gold medallist, felt he deserved Finance but could manage only Economic Affairs, while the missus, old-fashioned in her preferences, asked for and was given Home. They worked ten-hour days six days a week, and on Sundays there were always some social engagements, and the six newspapers they both read every day and television to follow. Master Sanjay Saran was thus left, more or less, to his own devices. The servants ensured he was fed and watered, and his mother made sure he never forgot that he had to come first in every test and exam – anything less was unacceptable.

So Sanju focused, worked hard and managed an 80 per cent in the dreaded subject and second position in class; Akku came first that year.

'I must say, for a slim, young fellow, Sanju is a real petu,' remarked Abha one evening after Sanju had left in his mother's official car at eight.

'What do you mean, Maasi,' protested Akku instantly. 'He doesn't eat that much!'

'Of course he does,' teased Abha. 'Ate up all the kebabs and a couple of chicken sandwiches to boot! And washed the lot down with two bottles of Coke.'

'You are so unfair,' replied Akku vehemently. 'Boys always eat more than girls anyway.'

'Hey, hey, easy there, child. I'm only teasing. Growing young men need more food than us girls, that's a fact. No need to pull a face just because I commented on your boyfriend's eating habits.'

'He's not my boyfriend! He's just my best friend and you keep making fun of him.'

'Okay, sorry. Now come on, help me clean up before your mother arrives and starts yelling at me too.'

Later that night over coffee and the late-night news, Abha mentioned Akku's little outburst to her sister.

'The boy spends all his free time here. It's a bit much. Akku seems to have no friend other than him. When Nandini came for a sleepover last week, she was laughing about it, said she was possibly

Akku's only friend other than Sanju. That's not good for Akku, ben.'

'Oh come on, they are both so young. No danger of anything untoward right now, is there? His parents must be working long hours and they don't have a family member with a fancy flexi-hours job like you to keep the boy company.'

'Christ, they are growing up so quickly, aren't they? Akku is almost ten and I bet her period will start soon – we all began early, if you remember. You got yours at nine, didn't you?'

'Nine and a half,' said Gayatri. 'God, it was miserable. Ba was horrified, but recovered quickly enough to guide me through it reasonably well. Well enough for that generation at least.'

'Yes, we've been lucky in our parents.'

'Indeed. Especially you! Any other set from that generation would have excommunicated you for your shenanigans!'

'Burnt me at the stake more likely!' said Abha.

'Looking back, I suspect Ba had some seriously wild genes that were kept in check by the times, circumstances and Pappa! And she passed them on to both of us. You've just put them in some freezer after Arjun bhai.'

Gayatri was quiet for a while.

'I didn't put anything away after Arjun died, Abha. One part of me just switched off with him. If it weren't for Akku and you, I would have followed him – I had a box of sleeping pills by my bedside for a long time.'

'Ben, that's insane! I had no idea!'

'I'm just telling you as it was. But don't worry, I pulled back from that place soon enough. Now I'm going to bed; I have some complicated procedures early tomorrow. Goodnight.'

Gayatri got up to leave, then yielding to a rare impulse stepped up to her sister and gave her a tight hug.

'Wow,' remarked Abha. 'And that was in honour of what, pray?'

'Why?' Gayatri asked from the door. 'I can't hug my sister now?'

'Not at all; you're welcome to, any time. It's just that you haven't in so many years that it was quite a shock,' Abha laughed.

'Yes, well, once every five years is enough, don't you think? We can't be getting all soppy and sentimental now, can we!' And with that, Gayatri went to her bedroom.

Abha turned on the TV but found it hard to focus on the latest offerings. She brooded instead. Something about Gayatri was different, something had changed, but Abha could not for the life of her figure out what. At midnight, she finally abandoned the reality show and went to bed in a rather troubled state of mind.

5

WHEN SIXTEEN-YEAR-OLD GAYATRI PATEL ANNOUNCED at the dinner table that she had decided to become a doctor, her parents were startled but took care not to show it. Dr Patel reached for a chapati and Mrs Patel offered him some dal, which he accepted. Only young Abha reacted quickly and vehemently as was her wont.

'How boring! You have to study for years and years and look at sick people all day – yuck!'

Dr Patel ignored his volatile young daughter's outburst and turned to his sober, studious and quiet elder progeny.

'Sudden decision, is it?' he asked.

'Oh no, Pappa, I've been thinking about it for a long time now. That's the only thing I want to do – become a doctor. Nothing else interests me.'

'Well, think about it carefully – there's no hurry. You have to dedicate about nine years of your youth to very hard work; no time for anything else at all. It's a very hard life and needs enormous commitment; without that you won't be able to manage the very tough regime You have to be sure you really and truly want to do this and it's not just some passing fancy.'

'Eight and a half years actually,' replied Gayatri. 'I've done my research, and I'm serious about it, totally serious.'

'Okay, fine then. But for now, get on with your ISC preparation. Get five points and we'll take a decision after the results are out.'

But it turned out Gayatri already had a plan.

'I've taken a decision, Pappa. I'll enroll for BSc (General) after ISC, and then I'll be eligible to take the Medical entrance after the first year. AIIMS is of course my first choice.'

Dr Patel looked up at his daughter impatiently. Doctor sahib was notoriously short-tempered with little patience for views contrary to his own.

Mrs Patel intervened very quickly.

'Abha, come on, help me clear the table. You two continue your discussion in the living room. Come along now, Abha, move.'

'I helped clear up yesterday – why can't ben do it today?' protested Abha immediately. Abha hated kitchen work of any sort and made her preferences clear at every opportunity. That, however, had no effect on her mother, who handed her a pile of used utensils.

'Go on, start rinsing them while I bring the rest.'

And Abha complied, reluctantly.

Dr Patel was an excellent diagnostician and therefore a very shrewd and good judge of people. He also doted on both his offspring, but hid it under a gruff and often distant manner.

When he and Gayatri were seated in the living room, he switched on the TV, settled on his favourite news channel, pressed the mute button in anticipation of the nine o'clock news and returned to the matter at hand.

'All I'm telling you, Gayatri, is to keep an open mind about your options and take a call after the ISC results are announced. Whatever you then decide, I will support you fully.'

Gayatri smiled. She knew her father well.

'Of course, Pappa. We'll discuss it then.'

Dr Patel concealed his approval of his daughter's strategic mind and turned his attention to the news programme. That was the moment, as he told his slightly distraught wife later in bed, when he realized that Gayatri had indeed reached a real decision and would definitely become a doctor.

'The entrance exam is very difficult, isn't it?' his wife ventured hopefully.

'Are you saying your daughter won't pass? I guarantee she will be amongst the top fifty and will get AIIMS. Two of my batchmates are professors there; I must re-establish contact with them.'

'When will she marry, when will she have children? This is no profession for a woman,' said Mrs Patel.

'Oh relax, will you? Nothing has happened yet, and you're going on as if the heavens have fallen. She will marry at thirty and have her children before she's thirty-five – no problem.'

But Mrs Patel was not to be placated and kept awake worrying about her daughter long after doctor sahib had fallen fast asleep, approximately a minute after his head touched the pillow.

The ISC exams came and went. Gayatri topped her school with seven points and joined the BSc (General) course, which met the pre-med requirement. As doctor sahib had predicted, his daughter ranked thirty-fifth in the state medical exam, qualified for admission to AIIMS and joined the august institution in her nineteenth year.

'Look how thin she has become,' complained her mother every time Gayatri came home during the holidays.

'I'm absolutely fit, Ba,' Gayatri would reply whenever the issue was raised. 'I eat healthy, I exercise and I work hard, very hard. And I do not need laddoos made in ghee. Anyway, every time I take them back, the boys eat them all. So your efforts are always wasted.'

'Any interesting boys, ben?' Abha would ask to disapproving stares from her mother. 'Any nice Gujju Patels, for example? Ba would be so thrilled.'

'Abha, you will get a smack for talking nonsense, if you continue like this,' threatened her mother but Abha only laughed. Their mother had not smacked either daughter in living memory; a word of disapproval was normally enough.

The years went by. Gayatri Patel graduated near the top of her class and started her internship as Abha turned sixteen and got embroiled in her first major scandal.

In the small Maharashtrian town where the Patels had been settled for several generations, there was a very active theatre group and Abha, since age thirteen, had been a star member and performer. Over the next three years she had grown into a strikingly attractive young woman and a very talented theatre actor. The group put up an adaptation of Ibsen's *A Doll's House* that was quite well received. The cast party that followed, however, provided large amounts of grist to the local gossip mills and Abha Patel featured prominently in the tales of shocking depravity that circulated soon thereafter. Rumour had it that a good deal of alcohol was consumed, even by some of the girls led by Abha, and a striptease had taken place, again with Abha as the principal performer. Apparently someone had seen her in a 'compromising position' with the handsome ne'er-do-well Rohit Malpani, who was in charge of the lights. Abha heard the gory details the next day and exploded with rage. Yes, they had consumed a fair amount of cheap vodka, and yes, they had danced. Nobody had taken any clothes off – a scarf dramatically cast aside and maybe a button or two unbuttoned, but that was all – she had simply indulged in a kiss and then pushed away an overeager Rohit Malpani and made her way to a girlfriend's home where she, as per plan, was to spend the night. There, in a girls-only group, they did dance to a few sexy item numbers but what the hell, not much by way of sin, was it?

'Which bitch leaked, I wonder?' asked Abha of her best friend and co-conspirator in the striptease, a young lady named Radhika. 'Bet it was that Rajalaxmi. She must have told her stupid brother and he, of course, announced it to the world.'

'It's reached my mom, can you believe it? Do your parents know?' asked Radhika.

'Not yet. What did your mom say?'

'Nothing much. Asked me what happened and I told her. She knows I don't lie to her, so she believed me. Just told me to have a little more sense in future and not drink with a bunch of 'ghatis'. Thank God we're moving to Bombay next month. These one-horse towns are really the pits!'

Abha rather liked her small town and the few close friends she had, but nodded agreement – it was nice, but stifling too.

'I'm applying everywhere – Delhi, Bombay, Oxford, New York – as soon as the results come. It's happening, folks!'

6

PUBERTY CAME EARLY TO AKKU. SHE STARTED menstruating three months short of her eleventh birthday. With both her mother and Abha available for guidance and counselling, the transition, both physical and emotional, was less problematic than one would expect. Sanju baba, however, like most young men, lagged a long way behind in the journey to psychological maturity.

'He's so stupid, Abha Maasi. I thought he would understand what I'm going through – we're best friends and we share everything – but he's not interested at all. He's forever lost in his stupid storybooks. And that silly Astha keeps talking to him all the time. And I've caught him staring at her boobs! She has bigger boobs than all the girls in class. Stupid girl!'

'Everyone's bodies work in different ways, Akku, especially now that all sorts of changes are taking place. Besides, it's really not important how big your boobs are!'

'You don't know anything, Maasi. The boys just want to hang around her all the time so they can enjoy the view,' Akku said crossly and marched away. Despite her recent concerns, however, her focus on her schoolwork did not waver. She still had to get first place and show Sanju just how stupid that cow Astha was – barely able to pass in Maths!

'I tell you, ben, I didn't know whether to laugh or cry. But danger time is nigh. As soon as that boy can get it up …'

'Abha, you are quite impossible,' replied Gayatri with a smile. 'But I agree, some thorough talking-to is required now. I've got this book I picked up in New York on my last visit. I'll hand it to her when we have our discussion this weekend.'

'You do it your way, I'll do it my way,' replied Abha and there the matter rested.

After Sanju made his first ill-fated attempt at physical intimacy in the cinema hall, Akku did not speak to him for two whole days. On the third day, she could not stand it any more and marched up to him during lunch break and said, 'If you say sorry and mean it, I'll start talking to you again. And I've got chicken sandwiches in the cold bag today – Maasi made them.'

The combination of Akku backing down and the chicken sandwiches was too much to resist. Sanju apologized sincerely, got more than his share of the sandwiches as a result and things returned to normal – almost. The newly discovered sexual tension was a little subdued for a while, especially since final exams were now imminent. But when the holidays started, things got complicated again.

All was fine to begin with. The Sarans went off to Nainital for two weeks and the Patels to a cottage in the hills near Almora that Abha had bought recently. A number of odd expats, Europeans mostly, had built cottages near Almora on a hill aptly named 'Cranks Ridge', where they lived quiet, contemplative lives in splendid isolation. One such cottage was put on sale when its elderly owner died and left it to a nephew in Scotland. The nephew did not take to these parts very well, and wanted a quick sale and early return home. Abha heard about the sale from a friend settled in Almora, drove up, fell in love with the two-up-two-down stone cottage with a patal roof, made the best offer her savings would allow and found herself the owner of a sturdily built, south-facing, utterly delightful dwelling that needed a great deal of expensive repair.

'I am now the proud owner of a lovely home and an empty bank account,' she announced on the phone to her sister. 'Catch the first train you can get and head over, ben. I'll pick you guys up at Kathgodam.

7

EVERYONE RETURNED TO STEAMING HOT DELHI SOON enough and Sanju baba became a permanent fixture at Akku's house immediately thereafter. His mother's chauffeur would drop him after breakfast and pick him up whenever one of the Sarans got back home from work, which was never before seven-thirty in the evening.

'I can't be a full-time chaperone, ben,' said Abha in despair after a week. 'I have to show my face in office a few days a week at least; there are meetings to attend, authors to meet. It's just not possible!'

'I know,' said Gayatri. 'You can't let this affect your work, Abha. We just have to leave them alone together and hope for the best. Pray that good sense ...'

Abha cut her sister short, '... triumphs over hormones? C'mon, big ben, when did that ever happen? But I'll have a talk with her in any case. Trust she has more sense than a certain young woman who was two months pregnant at her wedding not so long ago!'

'Just one and a half, please, and I was twenty-seven,' Gayatri protested.

'True, ben, but that's when they start nowadays. Can't do anything about that.'

Gayatri shook her head and returned to her book and Abha to the manuscript she was reading that Saturday evening.

The two ladies were right to worry; the hormones were indeed flowing fast and furiously and some deep snogging and heavy petting were the inevitable result. However, the walls of repression, inhibition and guilt stood strong – more so in young Sanju than Akku, if truth be told, and the summer passed without any breaches of virginity. When not cuddling, Sanju read *War and Peace* and Akku got her brown belt in karate. Summer ended and school reopened to all the stresses of the last two years before the dreaded twelfth board exams.

8

ONE EVENING WHEN EIGHT-YEAR-OLD AKKU HAD been put to bed and the sisters were having coffee and watching the news, Gayatri turned to Abha suddenly and asked, 'Can you look after Akku this Friday evening? Unless you have a date or something, of course.'

Abha gave her sister a searching look.

'Why? Do you have a date or something, ben? Where are you going on a Friday evening?'

'Yes, actually I do have a date. Or something,' replied Gayatri looking her flummoxed sister straight in the eye. Dr Gayatri Patel was nothing if not tough when she chose to be.

But Abha made a fast recovery.

'Brilliant! At long last! Come on, big ben, this is wonderful news – tell all!'

Gayatri looked at the TV with unseeing eyes, then shook her head impatiently.

'Open a bottle of wine – it's a long story and not easy to tell without some alcohol.'

A bottle was opened, wine poured and served remarkably quickly.

'Here you are, ben. Now tell.'

Gayatri took a healthy gulp, put the glass down and muted the TV.

'You've met him, Abby. Its Vishy, Dr Vishwanathan.'

'Oh you sly thing, of course I've met him! And once I even got a hint of something brewing and you sooo casually dismissed it out of hand that even I got taken in. Strong and quiet – I like it, ben, I like it; tell me more.'

'Okay, well, when I joined the MS programme, there were just three of us in General Surgery – Arjun, me and this doctor from Vellore, Vishwanathan. Everyone called him Vishy. Arjun, you know, was loud, outgoing, so happy-go-lucky. He didn't work very hard, but he was a good surgeon – he had good hands. And he was really good with people. Dr Tandon, our Head of Department – what a brilliant surgeon – was quite fond of him.'

Gayatri paused and Abha had the good sense to remain silent.

'Vishy, on the other hand, was a genius. A magician with the scalpel, quiet, meticulous and enormously hard-working. He topped every exam that came his way. All three of us became good friends very soon. I, of course, fell for Arjun like the proverbial ton of bricks. He was a complete charmer, could even charm a straight-laced, reserved sincere behenji like me out of my clothes and into his bed in just six months!'

'Good god, you wicked woman! Premarital sex, you of all people!' Abha said in mock horror. 'Ba would've had a fit if she knew.'

Gayatri smiled with enormous amusement.

'Ba was the first one to know, my dear child. She gently asked me within a month of my losing my virtue, if I was involved with anyone and what my – and his – intentions were. In fact, she warned me not to take any hasty decisions and to ensure I didn't get pregnant!'

'In those words? I can't believe it.'

'Almost! She was only a little indirect, if I remember right. But she didn't mess about either. I told her I was a doctor and could take care of myself and there the matter rested until the day I informed her and Pappa about our decision to get married. But that was when we'd finished our MS.'

'And I missed all the fun as I was off at Cambridge, working my butt off, swotting away in the library!'

Gayatri nodded.

'Of course. We did get some idea of your hard work. Not easy getting arrested and spending a night in jail in a foreign country. You're lucky they didn't deport you!'

'Ah, come on, ben. Not for drinking and sleeping in the park on a summer night. The Brits are more liberal than that!'

'That wasn't all that happened in the park that summer night was it, Abha?' asked Gayatri with a faint grin.

Abha grinned back.

'Not quite. And the Brits are even more tolerant on that subject, by the way. The last thing they said to us when they turned us out of the police station in the morning was to find a nice warm room for it in future and not shock the elders taking a quiet stroll after dinner.'

'You mad thing! Whatever possessed you to do it in the park, for heaven's sake?'

'It was just the perfect setting, and we both felt the urge, that's all. But we're straying, dear sister. The topic is your Friday night shenanigans. So go on, start at the beginning, go to the end and then stop.'

Gayatri drained her glass and refilled it.

'Vishy and Arjun were best friends from the beginning of the course and I joined them very soon. The work was brutal and I suspect Vishy helped Arjun out a lot. Anyway, in six months Arjun and I were together and time passed rather quickly. I always admired Vishy, but never looked at him in any romantic light – I was too obsessed with Arjun! And then the MS was finally over and we got careless and pregnant and married and I was ready to live happily ever after.'

Gayatri paused and had a sip of her drink.

'But the fairy tale ended there. I got the job at the Institute – there was only one vacancy – Akku was born, and Arjun started drinking more than usual. But we were working things out; Arjun got a job at that fancy private hospital and we would've been fine, I have no doubt. But we never got the chance. He'd just finished a complicated procedure, washed up, changed and got back to his room when the attack happened.

They found him half an hour later, when a colleague walked in to chat about something. But, you know all that ... They tried everything – they have some very fancy facilities – but he'd been dead for a while. So there I was, a demanding job, a six-month-old baby and a dead husband.'

Abha cleared her throat, drained her glass and refilled it.

'That's when Ba came over to stay and you started working insane hours, right?'

'Yes. I took three weeks off and went home, but Pappa agreed when I said I needed to get to work or I'd go mad. So, back I came with Ba and baby in tow. Ba stayed for six months, then I sent her back. Poor Pappa, managing the house by himself! Of course, he made frequent trips – he was cutting down on his practice anyway – he'd stopped seeing new patients after his first heart attack.'

'And what about Dr Vishwanathan?'

'Yes, Vishy was the rock on which I leaned through all this. All the paperwork got done because he knew someone in every office. I just signed papers and he took them away and things happened. He found me a maid for Akku, he did everything, even handled

Arjun's parents when they came for the funeral. They, of course, blamed me, or my 'bad mangal', for his death. Thank God they've had nothing to do with me ever since.'

Gayatri looked at the wall clock and got up abruptly.

'It's late and I have work early tomorrow. We'll talk later, Abha.'

'Oh no, you don't, ben! You can't leave me hanging like this, sorry. Finish the darn story! What and when did things change, who pushed whom and how? Out with it.'

'Vishy didn't push me at all; he was just there for me all these years. But over time, in a very gentle way, he made it clear that he was waiting for me to come around and take a decision. He's very perceptive and knew that I was just switched off in some way and needed some time before I could take a call on our relationship. There were no deep conversations or epiphanies, but over the last six months I realized that I had surfaced in some sense, and wanted him as more than a friend. He sensed the change and things moved forward, slowly but surely. And now I'm done. I can't verbalize like you writer types. I'm off to bed.'

'Sure, but at least tell me where you're going on Friday night?'

'Oh, Vishy has discovered some new Italian joint in Defence Colony. We're going to check it out.'

'And for coffee to his place, I trust?'

Gayatri just smiled at her sister, got up and left.

'Hope to Christ this works out for you, ben of mine,' muttered Abha to herself as she cleared up and retired for the night. 'About time the bloody stars turned in your favour.'

9

'YOU'RE MAD, SANJU, YOU REALLY ARE!' EXCLAIMED Akku as she examined the contents of a large cardboard box sitting on Sanju's hostel room floor.

'Oh come on, Akku. My nana saved all the letters I had written to him and when he died, my mother went to his house to settle his affairs and found them, that's all,' replied Sanju impatiently.

'And instead of tearing them up, carefully saved up all her little genius' writings, right? Amazing. And you've preserved them too, I notice. Get you the first Nobel, will they?'

'You're really being bitchy today, aren't you?' protested Sanju.

'No, dude. Just pointing out that not every word you write is worth preserving. But, yes, I'm totally not in the mood so, no, I won't reconsider. You push too much and I'm warning you I'll bite it off!'

Sanju took a deep breath and held his peace. It was hard dealing with a no, but there was really no option when Akku was in such a mood.

Silence reigned as Sanju pretended to read *Finnegans Wake* and Akku sampled the letters saved carefully by a doting grandfather and mother.

'You had lovely handwriting even at age eight, but you wrote like a stuck-up prick then too!' observed Akku.

'And you always had filthy writing and still cannot string together three coherent sentences in English, or any other language for that matter!' retorted Sanju heatedly.

Akku laughed and leaned over to give her boyfriend a tight hug.

'You really get tetchy when you don't get any, don't you, babe? Men are always horny and women often moody and uninterested – rules of life, my dear. Get used to it.'

'Life is tough,' acknowledged Sanju as he hugged her back. 'We need our greens regularly, you know, necessary for health.'

'Yeah, sure! So is occasional abstinence. Oh, did I tell you I've applied for a three-month internship this summer? The Big Three of software each offer one position at one of their development centres in the US. Very high-profile. You get to work with top design groups, get paid a nice amount of money and if you impress them, you may just get a job offer.'

'What are the criteria for selection?'

'Grades till date and an interview. Mine's next week.'

'With your grades, you are a sure shot, Akku. And that means I'll be on my own all summer. Oh God.'

Akku hugged him again, then sat back with a thoughtful expression. 'Actually, if I do get it, we will be apart all summer for the first time in what, fifteen years! Shit, never thought about that.'

'It's too much, yaar, all summer,' groaned Sanju.

'Yeah, a no-nookie summer, lover boy. Start studying for the UPSC as your dad suggested. Or go hiking in the Himalayas and read all the Dostoevsky and Shakespeare that you haven't already read. Take your pick.'

'I'll have to start working for the UPSC, baby, no option. My dad's enrolling me in one of those classes that have a good track record, according to his researches. He's already decided on the papers I'm going to take, drawn up reading lists and marked off the ones for which he'll make notes! He's nothing if not thorough, that's for sure. And they're both getting posted back to Delhi soon – a couple of months at most. My days of freedom are over.'

'You sound a little bitter, buddy, instead of bloody grateful as you should be! They take so much interest in you – be happy.'

'Yeah, I know,' replied Sanju, sounding rather unconvinced. 'They'll insist I shift home for the final year of the MA and prep for the UPSC. How will we ever meet?'

'Ah, now I get it. Don't worry – remember the old song "Love will find a way"?' Akku said, cooing into his ear. 'We've managed before, we'll manage again, lover, fear not.'

'You don't know, Akku, you have no idea,' muttered Sanju. 'C'mon, let's go get samosas and nimbu paani, I'm starving.'

What Sanju didn't tell Akku was that he still wrote to his nana, only now it was in his head, not on paper. His nana was the only person Sanju could spill his guts to, and he did so when something troubled him.

And recently there was a great deal that was troubling him.

10

THE MUCH-AWAITED FRIDAY EVENING CAME AROUND and Dr Gayatri Patel-Bansal got home early from work. Abha was waiting impatiently.

'You need time to get dressed and it's already six. What time is he picking you up?'

'Eight-thirty; plenty of time, Abha. I need a cup of tea and a quick shower – more than enough time. Now what's your dinner plan?'

'Akku and I are treating ourselves to pizza and ice cream, preceded by Coke and TV for her and a glass of wine for me. The TV's on already so don't you worry, focus on the evening; we'll be fine.'

'Good. Forget the tea, I'll just go and shower. Then you can help me decide what to wear and give me a small whiskey before Vishy arrives.'

Abha nodded approval. If big ben was asking for a whiskey, things were looking up indeed. Adventure was in the air.

'I have something for you,' she said, and produced a large bag from which she pulled out a black handloom salwar-kurta with a touch of blue piping and a dramatic silk chunni, turquoise with black embroidery. Gayatri was both touched and amused, and agreed to wear the outfit, but firmly rejected the notion of doing without a bra.

'All your yoga has kept you beautifully toned, ben – they are still firmly defying gravity! C'mon, be brave, give him a thrill!'

'Hush, Abha. I've a lacy black one somewhere that should do well enough; just find it for me, will you? And, if you don't mind, I give him a thrill regardless of what I am or am not wearing.'

'Whoops, that was a straight left to the chin. Good for you. Now get into the kurta and let's have a look at the final result.'

'It's too loud, too young,' protested Gayatri and Abha lost it just a little bit.

'For heaven's sake, you're thirty-seven not eighty-seven, darling. Relax, you look spectacularly sophisticated and sexy, and if he has any balls he should simply grab you and do you in the car! Oh Christ, don't look so tense, just chill, ben, relax and go with the flow. And here's your whiskey. I've opened the Laphroaig so sit and sip while I decide on the perfume you'll wear.'

Gayatri did as told while Abha selected and drenched her sister with the perfume of her choice.

'Here, there and yonder – you never know where he might end up.'

Gayatri smiled at her sister with enormous affection. 'You need to find a nice man, Abha, not these temps you make do with. Then you'll realize that none of this matters a damn.'

'True, true, sister dear. But all the nice ones are married and "the mere lees is left this vault to brag of –"'

'Doesn't quite fit, does it?'

'I always forget you've read a few books. And yes, it doesn't, but it was the best I could do on the spur of the moment!'

The sisters sat quietly together, one a little nervous, the other silently thrilled, till Dr Vishwanathan arrived at the door and Gayatri left.

11

'YOU LOOK STUNNING, GAYATRI,' SAID Dr Vishwanathan as he drove carefully away from the Bansal house.

'Thank you, Vishy. But you could be a little less matter-of-fact about it, you know,' Gayatri replied, smiling just a little.

'True. But I do have to drive and this is Delhi traffic, you see,' said Vishy quietly, composed as always.

'Okay, so how about telling me where we're going this evening? Are we still set on Italian?'

'We go wherever you want to go, G.'

'I'm not hungry. Take me home, please, Vishy.'

'Oh okay, let me make a U-turn at the next –'

'Not my house, Vishy,' Gayatri interrupted. 'Just take me home.'

Dr Vishwanathan was silent as he changed course and drove towards his Greater Kailash residence.

'And say something, for heaven's sake, don't make me do all the talking.'

Vishy laughed softly.

'You are quite wonderful, my dear G, and I'm no good with words, as you well know. So wait for a while for me to ... er ... effectively convey my feelings.'

Gayatri laughed in return and gently patted his knee.

'Effectively' is a good word, Vishy. Now drive carefully; I can wait.'

They entered Vishy's house in silence; he shut the door behind them and switched on the lights.

'Very nice, Vishy, very nice indeed,' remarked Gayatri, after a careful look around the sparse, but very aesthetically furnished room. 'Did this yourself, did you? And never invited me to visit either!'

Vishy reached out, gripped her hands in his and they looked at each other quietly for a while. Then Gayatri pulled her hands free, stepped up close and put her arms around his neck.

'All yours, Vishy,' she said with a smile, and all the inhibitions in place for almost a decade collapsed and they were just two new lovers, though no longer young, reaching out to each other after years of restraint.

They were skilled senior surgeons, both of them, so despite hammering hearts and heavy breathing, they managed a modicum of control. They kissed tentatively at first and, as inhibitions crumbled, urgently. They came up for air after a while, grinned at each other and moved to the bedroom where they kissed again, undressed and finally found themselves naked in bed.

Vishy turned on a lamp on the side table.

'I want to see you, Gayatri, if you permit.'

'Yes, permitted,' she said, a trifle breathlessly. 'And throw that silly condom away and hold me, please.'

Vishy complied.

'You have to help me a little here,' he murmured, stroking her slim back and firm buttocks with long firm strokes.

Gayatri turned over on her back.

'You've studied as much anatomy as I have, doctor,' she said with a smile, 'so do something, everything, please, and don't stop!'

A good while later, after a more than satisfactory finale, Gayatri shook her somnolent lover awake.

'Hey, Vishy, I'm hungry. Anything in the fridge?'

'Yes. Stay right there, I'll fix something.'

In five minutes Vishy returned with sandwiches and wine.

'You didn't make these now, so quickly, Vishy?'

Vishy smiled and shook his head.

'Advance planning. One has to plan for all contingencies, right, doctor?'

'You wicked, wicked man. Not that I mind such impressive efficiency. And you of course will drink water and ice, as always?'

'Need all my wits about me with a strange woman in my bed.'

'Strange?!'

'I meant wonderful, of course. And very sexy, too.'

'Good to hear that! But I should get going soon, Vishy – it's late.'

'Stay over, G. I'll drop you home early, before Akku wakes up.'

Gayatri took a sip of the wine, thought for a while, then looked up with a smile.

'Fine, I didn't really want to go, just thought I should. I'll call Abha – she'll be waiting.'

12

Dear Nana,

Growing up is terrible. The first year of my MA is almost over, as is my freedom to do as I wish. I want to write an obscure thesis on Ivy Compton-Burnett, make love to Akku and teach introductory courses on Jane Austen and Shakespeare at some small private college on the eastern seaboard of the US. Instead, I'll be joining a second-rate – intellectually speaking – coaching class that will teach me how to pass the UPSC and hopefully get into the IAS (anything else will be a serious blow to my parents) and be a sahib for the rest of my life. A few years in the state, then on to Delhi like my parents: a deputation to the UN and a house in suburban Noida for my retirement. God, the mere thought is terrifying! But that is my future, if I am lucky.

Besides, does one have the right to do as one wishes if it means breaking one's parents' hearts? Or should I give myself a break and be a little indulgent? But what if I'm wrong and end up as a complete failure, miss out on all the promised rank and stature that a Services job will bring? I really don't know what to do, Nana, and you no longer reply to my letters anyway. Chalo, Dad is back and dinner will soon be served.

Yours,
Sanju

~

Dear Nana,

Dad is impossible! I don't know how Mummy has tolerated him all these years. He has a fixed view on everything and any dissent, and dissenter, is ignorant and stupid. Everyone has to do as he says, because he knows best and that's the end of the matter. God, I wish I could just pack a bag and walk out! Instead, all I can do is vent. I've had to move out of the hostel, as they've got a nice big house in Pandara Park, and now meeting Akku is extremely difficult – too many servants in the house at almost every waking hour, even if the parents are not.

I've joined Aiyyar's coaching classes and three days a week I go there straight from college. Dad is making notes in History for me; he starts after dinner and stays up half the night, and in the morning I have a neat pile of papers waiting for me at the breakfast table.

Akku is off to California for three months – that's all summer. What am I going to do? And I wonder what she'll be up to there – mainly hard work, I hope!

Bye for now. I have to go back to mugging up all sorts of silly facts that pass for GK in our exam system!

Sanju

~

Dear Nana,

Saw Akku off at the airport last night. Her mom and maasi were there too. She was so excited and not too bothered that I'll be all by myself here. I'm very upset of course, but what the hell, we all have our compulsions, I guess.

Dad appears quite pissed off with me this morning, I wonder why.

Anyway, back to the salt mines.

Bye,

Sanju

~

Dear Nana,

Dad is raving mad at me – the telephone bill, after all those calls to Akku, has arrived! I didn't realize it would be so much, honest. And anyway, what's the point of being a big shot in government if you have to bother about trivial stuff like a couple of thousand rupees in international calls! I mean, these are people running this damned country, for God's sake. They've dedicated their lives to managing this circus and still they have to answer to some bloody babu in accounts for things like telephone calls. No bloody soap-selling CEO would ever be subject to such an insult, I tell you! And people wonder why things are going down the tubes here.

My coaching class is truly terrible – full of small-town wannabes actually thinking they can govern this country and they can't even put together three consecutive sentences in English right!

Anyway, got to go – have an assignment to finish.

Bye,

Sanju

Dear Nana

I'm very, very upset. Akku is having a great time in sunny California and I'm stuck here mugging for this stupid exam. She sent me pictures of her on the beach with her gang of computer geniuses. And she was wearing a tiny black bikini for crying out loud, all these tall American guys all about her. I just don't like it, Nana. I don't want her going out with all those guys and I don't want her so far away from me; I don't want to be sucked into this sarkari tamasha that I've been born into. I just want to be with Akku in California and oh god, I'm just fed up with all of this, totally and completely fed up. I shudder to think in twenty years' time I'll be just like my father. AAARRGGGHHH!

Bye for now,

Sanju

13

'STICK TO SURGERY, BEN, LEAVE CHILD PSYCHOLOGY alone, you know nothing about it,' said Abha.

'And you of course are an expert, aren't you?' asked Gayatri with a smile. 'My in-house expert on child-rearing.'

Abha shook her head in exasperation and poured more tea for herself and her sister. The morning tea–newspaper–chat session was a weekend ritual for the sisters; everything from the state of the nation to the misdemeanours of the house help was discussed. Abha's insistence on talking about Gayatri's suddenly blossoming love life, was, however, not proceeding very smoothly.

'I can't upset her whole view of the world at this stage, Abha. She has you and me and this house and a pattern of life. She's just hit puberty, that's disturbance enough; she doesn't need to learn that her mother has a boyfriend and goes off with him for some strange, unknown reason at odd hours. Let some time pass, let her grow up a little.'

'And you two will just sneak around like teenagers while she grows up – is that the plan? And what does your boyfriend have to say about it all?'

'It's my daughter and my decision. Besides, did no one ever tell you that love can be tough? Just FYI, it can. Very. Tough.'

Abha took a deep breath and dunked a biscuit in her tea.

'I still disagree. Kids are strong and understand a great deal more than you think. Anyway, your kid, your decision, like you said. I'm a good soldier; I obey orders and do as I am told.'

Gayatri laughed out loud at this pious proclamation.

'Yes, that's the saintly little sister I've known all these years! So here's an order: find a nice man and settle down, soon. And it's your turn to do breakfast today. I'm off to get ready.'

Sunday mornings passed at an easy pace in the Patel sisters' household. Akku watched TV after a late breakfast, got dressed and then waited impatiently for

Abha to emerge from her room and take her out for her drawing workshop and a late lunch. Gayatri had other plans: an afternoon at Vishy's, a cosy stay-in lunch, and evening at home with Akku while Abha went out partying.

14

WHEN AKKU CLEARED THE IIT ENTRANCE EXAM AND got into its Delhi institute to study Computer Science, her mother and aunt took her out for dinner, bought her a state-of-the-art laptop, and one quiet evening before classes were to start, Gayatri told her about Dr Vishwanathan.

She had planned her words carefully, rehearsed them over and over again till it was finally time. She sat her daughter down beside her, held her hand and said her piece, then looked at Akku in anticipation of a reaction she was sure would be violent, one way or another.

Akku heard her mother out in silence, a silence that stretched for a while after Gayatri had finished. Then she turned to her mother, put her arms around her and wept.

Both mother and daughter cried for a while and then Gayatri dried her eyes and gently stroked her daughter's thick, unruly hair.

'Come on now, Akku, it's not that bad, is it? Or are you totally angry with me?'

Akku's sniffles returned; she used her mother's pallu to dry her eyes and gave Gayatri a tight hug.

'Of course I'm a little shocked, Mummy. Whenever Vishy uncle came over, you acted so weird – I always wondered what on earth was going on. But now I know, I'm so, so happy for you. And I'm seriously angry that you hid it from me and obviously have been sneaking around all these years just to, what, protect me? Jesus, Mummy! I'm a fricking millennial, an adult at that; you could've told me and lived a more normal life!'

Gayatri smiled and returned her daughter's embrace.

'Of course you are, Akku, and your reaction is an adult one too! Let's just say my decision was old-fashioned and dumb, but then I've done the right thing now, haven't I?'

'Yeah. So, are you guys going to get married. Or what?'

Gayatri took a deep breath and patted her daughter's hand.

'One thing at a time, child. To begin with, he's taking us all out for dinner tomorrow. How does that sound?'

'Awesome!' exclaimed Akku, hugged her mother yet again and got up to leave.

'I have to talk to Sanju. The DU lists will be out any day now and the poor guy's in a real tizzy. If he doesn't get Stephen's his parents might just disown him. Thank god for a mom like you!'

Akku went back to her room as Abha emerged from hers – where she had diplomatically withdrawn for the last hour – opened a bottle of wine and handed a full glass to her sister.

Gayatri drained her glass in three gulps and wordlessly handed it over for a refill.

'That bad, huh?' said Abha.

'No, not really. Rather good, in fact. What a composed eighteen-year-old! She said she was happy for me and asked if we were getting married!'

'Wow, she's moving faster than you!'

'I don't know ... let's just hope she can actually deal with it as well as she appears to be doing.'

'Yes, indeed. But I'm glad you had the talk. It was time. We'll keep a close watch on Akku, make sure she remains more or less on even keel. Now relax, and drink up! Your daughter is a sound person, doctor, and we've done a fair job of bringing her up. Cheers!'

Gayatri smiled and gently punched her sister's shoulder.

'We've done our best, at any rate. And that's all one can hope to do. Cheers, darling sister!'

'And thank the lord she has your genes – both looks and brains and five foot five to boot! But she must somehow get out of this Sanju obsession of hers. I was hoping she would grow out of it with time but that's yet to happen.'

'Why do you dislike him so much, Abha? He's a nice enough boy – intelligent, polite, and quite well behaved. Soon they'll be off to college and things will change, I presume.'

'And if they don't?'

'Well, then, let's hope it will turn into something serious and worth encouraging.'

'I don't know, ben, something about it makes me uncomfortable. Theirs is a different world, you know. Remember the time I took Akku to his birthday party years ago? I spent more than two hours in their flat – broad roads outside, huge parks, very different from the diesel fumes of Aurobindo Marg I can assure you! And a lot of condescension and arrogance to go with it all.'

'Oh come on, Abha. You've always been too sensitive anyway. And we have a green and peaceful oasis of our own here, too.'

'True, but the screeching traffic, the dust, the fumes, the crowds – all just a minute away! Lutyens' Delhi is something else again, ben, you can't deny it. It's the seat of entitlement and privilege – they rule, they don't protect and serve. And when they get their next Delhi postings, young Sanju's parents will be senior enough for Pandara Park – even quieter, even more green and insulated from the hoi polloi. I'm telling you, ben, it's a world we don't really know and wouldn't like if we did.'

'God knows what you've been reading these days, Abha, but that's more negativity than I can handle in one day, so let's have another drink.'

15

THE LAST TEST WAS THE TOUGHEST, BUT AKRITI finished ten minutes early, checked her work, submitted her paper and walked out the door two minutes before the bell rang. She walked alone to her hostel, dumped her jhola on her desk and lay down on the bed – it had been a hectic fortnight of nose to the grindstone, countless mugs of coffee and minimal sleep; she was dead beat.

At six-thirty, Laxmi banged on the door. She was the oldest student in the hostel, a PhD candidate in the Material Science department, in the final stages of her thesis, and Akku's newest friend. Institute gossip maintained that she had been offered admission by a fancy Ivy League university after her MSc, but had turned it down and joined the IIT instead, all for the love of a bright young assistant professor. People insisted they had been living together, until one day the young man announced that he was getting married and moving to a small state university in the US where his would-be father-in-law was a professor.

Laxmi, however, displayed no symptoms of a broken heart, remained cheerfully profane always, published two important papers in leading international journals and slowly became the 'wise aunt' figure for the lovesick ladies in the hostel.

'Get your butt up, Snorkriti! I could hear you all the way from my room.'

Akku woke with a start, opened the door and went straight back to bed.

'I don't snore,' was her only comment.

'You do too, and as loudly as my stomach's growling this very moment. Are we going to get your post-test fix or what?'

The fix was usually a plate of momos followed by the famous fried rice and chicken manchurian at Ching's Chinese Corner across the road from the Institute's main gate.

Ramprasad Tiwari, the owner and head chef at Ching's, welcomed them – they were regular customers – and yelled the usual order to his assistant slaving behind the stove.

'So, off for the weekend, huh, you lucky thing!' observed Laxmi. 'And you aced the test today, I bet?'

'Yes to both, mere dost, but man, that was some headscratcher. Arun sir isn't messing around. His courses are a major pain, I tell you.'

'Arun's one of the best in the business,' said Laxmi. 'One of the few profs who're actually at the cutting edge of their field, along with my beloved Sharmaji of course. The rest are all doing timepass, bless them.'

'But Lax, if Prof Sharma is so good what's he been doing here for all these years?'

'He was going to get tenure at Rutgers, did you know? Came back to get married, returned with his bride who never warmed to the US. Just couldn't adjust, for some strange reason. They stuck it out for a couple of years, then chucked it all and came back to her comfort zone – sadda Dilli. Luckily the twins were born in the States. As soon as they could, they formalized their US citizenship and went off to college in Maryland, leaving Sharmaji and spouse in good old Hauz Khas. Good for me though, I got a leading world authority in my field right here to guide me. Anyway, what's cooking this weekend? Sanju waiting with open arms and equipment at the ready I bet?'

Akku giggled. 'Anyone tell you, you're a dirty pig, Laxmi?' she asked.

'Sure, everyone. But aren't his parents going to be home for the weekend?'

'Wrong,' said Akku, grinning from ear to ear. 'His dad is in Brussels and his mum's busy preparing for some major conference – practically living in the office I hear!'

'Wonderful. So you'll be sore all week.'

'Shut up, Lax! I'll be spending a lot of time with my mom and aunt too. There's always these fancy things to eat with Abha Maasi around; food is as important as sex, you see.'

'You're a lucky girl, AK, you don't know how lucky. You found your man in kindergarten! Look at us, almost thirty and still looking!'

Akku bit into a momo, washed it down with a swallow of nimbu soda and took a deep breath.

'What's with the heavy sighs and boob thrusts? You have a problem you want to talk about?'

Akku moodily demolished another momo.

'We've grown up together, you know, Sanju and me. We've been through it all together.'

'So? Getting bored or what? Feel like a new man hunk?'

'No way, yaar – I think I'm in it for life. But suppose he gets bored? We've both changed a great deal over the years. Suppose we grow apart or something ... I don't know.'

'What a wise little twenty-one-year-old! But why this drama? Has he been acting weird lately or something?'

'Nothing I've noticed, but you know, just have these thoughts popping into my head now and then ...'

'Continue.'

'Well, we have very different family backgrounds. My immediate family's mostly all doctors, and the relatives all Gujju businessmen and their devoted wives. His parents attend meetings and briefings with ministers and the PM, while my uncles and cousins are busy bribing the local municipality inspectors or some such ...'

'What shit, yaar! Such unadulterated crap! Your mom's one of the top surgeons in her field, your aunt, a senior editor at the biggest publishing house in the country and you're a certified whizkid at the best technical institute in India! No need to sell yourself so short. In fact, you should think twice before shacking up with a godforsaken babu from a long line of babus who, if not personally corrupt, have spent their lives sucking up to corrupt and venal politicians to ensure their own privileged, entitled lives. Fuck it all, Akriti, don't get taken in by the sarkari narrative. Besides, if things are fine between the two of you everything else sort of adjusts – one way or another. Okay, rant over.'

'Wow, Lax!' Akku clapped her hands. 'Point taken, but their world is just not the same as ours. And they think very little of our world, that's slowly becoming clear to me.'

'All very well, AK, but have you at least talked to Sanjay about all this?'

'I'm not totally sure where he stands. To be honest, it's been bugging me a little, Lax. And now I'll be off to the US and he'll be miserable without me – he's whining already. At least his mom and dad will have their precious son all to themselves. God knows what they'll do to my poor Sanju.'

16

From: Akriti Bansal <akkuthepatel@abcmail.com>
To: Abha Patel <abhaedits@abcmail.com>

Dear Abha Maasi,

Summer's almost over and it's been wonderful! I learnt a great deal and the people here also learnt just how good we Indians are, you know – not just GUI makers and software testers like those so-called developers thronging the streets of Bangalore. By the time I get back, I'll have a job offer from one of the big three – will give you the name later when it's a sure thing. They're starting a development centre in Noida and when they do, I shall work for them as a solutions architect – a novice of course, but how exciting is this! The formal offer will come from their India office by month end. I've just shot off a mail to Sanju and you are the next to know. I'll text Mummy – she has no time for emails as usual. How are things with her and Vishy uncle? Please tell her how happy I am – Dr V is wonderful. Anyway, I don't intend to waste so much time. I'm going to grab and hogtie Master Sanju as early as possible. Let him get through the UPSC and before he goes for training, I want it done and dusted – too many matchmaking mamas wander around their training institute in Mussoorie! And just between you, me and the lamp post, yours truly got seriously propositioned by three hot Californians, all within one week. Every time it was on the beach at sunset, but worry not, every time I told them off gently because they are all very nice guys, and one of them is a brainy hunk at that! If I tell Sanju, he'll have a jealous hissy fit and I can't deal with that right now, especially when I firmly kept temptation at bay. Men can be so, so stupid. Anyway, time to grab lunch with the brainiac. See you in three weeks!

Love,

Akku

~

'I'm seriously worried about Akku, ben,' said Abha, as the sisters sat with coffee after dinner, waiting for the nightly news on TV. 'This thing of hers has gone on very long and she's taken its permanence for granted.'

Gayatri sighed. 'I know you have doubts about Sanjay's commitment, Abha.'

'For God's sake, ben, they're twenty-one! Men don't think commitment at this age – they think sex. He's a polite, introverted, and dare I say, selfish young man who's had a hot chick like your worthy daughter as girlfriend since kindergarten. He's got it all on a platter and hasn't needed to look around and make any effort at all. If he passes the Civils, he'll have a host of very eligible proposals and a set of ambitious parents pushing him in the caste- and community-appropriate direction, believe you me! And he doesn't have the gumption to resist. He's a fucking lalloo. Like most bloody Indian men. Your Vishy, with complete commitment, is a rare specimen and not easy to find, I assure you, from extensive personal experience.'

'Yes, I suppose I'm a lucky girl, and one who worries about you. And now you're getting me worried about Akku, too. But I don't know what to do.'

'Nothing to do at the moment. He's in college, no formal move makes any sense at this stage. But as soon as he gets a job, I suggest you ask him to make his intentions clear. No other option.'

Gayatri shook her head doubtfully.

'I don't know. It may be better to leave it to the kids to take a call. They started it, they have to resolve it. Anyway, there is time to think things through, we have a year to work on this.'

Abha made a face, finished her coffee and got to her feet.

'I could be wrong but I thought you should know I've been feeling uneasy. Our little girl is overcommitted. She really hasn't learnt anything from me. Play the field and wait ... and wait.'

17

Dear Nana,

The die is cast, the Prelim results just came in, I've got through and I will be taking the Civil Services Mains in October. My preparations are well in hand. Papa has completed reading and making notes for the History paper and I'm working on Eng Lit. The timing of the exam is perfect. I'll pick up my MA coursework after the Mains are over and hope to get a good degree by the end of the academic year. Don't worry, Plan B is in place, but it's definitely the second option now.

Akku has been away and will be back only at the end of August. She's going on a backpacking trip with some of her new friends after her internship gets over. All these years I've been used to having her around more or less all the time – quite clingy she used to be. That appears to be changing and I guess it's for the better – we have to grow up some time.

I've been brooding over some things the past few months and I'm beginning to see that real life is more compelling than fantasy, however attractive the latter may be. The thought of an academic career appears curiously tame now. I'd much rather do things to change the world than sit around in detached academia, reflecting on ideas. I see the way my parents have worked all their lives – the dedication, the commitment – and I marvel at how they've kept it up for so little in return, materially speaking. Their college batchmates who did MBAs and have been selling soap or toiletries are millionaires with fancy houses and huge cars and the pimps in the media grudge bureaucrats their piddly perks! I think that's just not fair. But the satisfaction of having contributed to transforming our backward society and economy is, I feel, way more than earning some obscene amount of money.

Anyway, I have begun to see my parents' point of view now. I agree that we have an 'extractive state' and a semi-feudal society dominated by long-established vested interests, but one can either lament the state of the nation or do something to change it! Increasingly I'm coming round to the view that actions speak louder than words and to do is to be. Fine words don't matter much. And so, I really hope I make it through and carry on the family tradition.

Got to get back to work.

Bye for now,

Sanju

~

From: Akriti Bansal <akkuthepatel@abcmail.com>
To: Abha Patel <abhaedits@abcmail.com>

Dear Abha Maasi,

I've been a little worried this past month. It's Sanju's emails – he sounds a little different, like not everything is okay. He just doesn't like my being away and meeting anybody – especially men – other than him! Part of me feels quite flattered but I'm also irritated at his insecurity and childishness. Are men really this stupid?

I called him the other day and he was so rude and distant, so I got snappy too and we had a fight. We made up, of course, the next day, but he's behaving like a complete asshole! I told him as much and he wasn't amused. I wish I hadn't agreed to go on this backpacking trip. I should just get back. But life will change now as soon as I start working and he ramps up preparations for his exam. God knows how we'll handle all the tensions.

I know it's the whole UPSC thing that's getting on his nerves – the exam, my being away and his parents getting on his case. His dad makes notes for him, can you believe it? Aaarghh, I might just cancel my backpacking trip and come right back, but I really want to see a little of America. Who knows when I'll get the chance again. Anyway, let's see ... I'll let you know how things pan out.

Much love,

Akku

~

Dear Nana,

Akku's back – yesss! She came over the other day after my parents had left for work. I shouldn't be telling you this, but not much you can do, so here: we spent almost the whole day in bed! God, was I drained by the end of it and she wanted to go for a walk of all things! Women, I tell you!

But she seems a little different after her time in the US. She jogs every morning and has joined a yoga class at work. She's started at some ridiculous salary – seriously high – and has little time now, except for weekends, when Mummy and Papa are home. You'll get a shock if you hear how much she's earning, especially when you compare it with the Civil Services scales. Imagine, for running the damn country you are paid a pittance and for helping some baniya sell his freaking groceries you're showered with a fortune. And then the bloody media cribs about bureaucratic perks, for heaven's sake! Semi-literates who couldn't find a better job now sit in judgement and get taken seriously. The whole bloody situation sucks is all I can say. In the old days, sarkari incomes were much higher, I'm told, and there was some well-deserved izzat for what one was doing. Thank God it's not all gone to the dogs yet.

Anyway, got to get down to work – am competing with a tidal wave of vernacs; they're totally choking the system these days.

Bye for now,
Sanju

~

'I don't know, Maasi, I can't understand it,' said Akku to her aunt, as they were out for a walk early one morning at the Lodhi Gardens. 'Sanju is so tense about the exam and he takes it all out on me. He obviously doesn't like that I'm working, thinks I'm overpaid and keeps oscillating between fear that he won't make it and a sort of assumption that he will. He just appears so angry with everything and everyone, especially me. It doesn't help that we have no time or place to be together these days – and I'm tired of going to the crowded Hauz Khas cafes! It's all very disturbing. I just hope he gets through and after his training we can get married – that should sort things out. I'm already trying to figure out how I can work from home – when the time comes – wherever that may be. I'll have to take a pay cut of course, but that's not such a big deal. I just want us to be together!'

18

Vishy was away at a conference and Akriti at her college hostel swotting for a major test. The sisters had themselves to each other on this pleasant Sunday morning with a chance of rain.

'It's been so long since we did this, no, ben?' said Abha, pouring the morning's first mugs of tea.

'Too long!' said Gayatri. 'And to think that so much has happened in our lives but I still don't know how you and Mo came to meet.'

'Well, you have to talk to me to find out, darling! Ever since Akriti was in middle school, Vishy's taken up all your time!'

'For heaven's sake, Abha!' said Gayatri with a smile.

'Oh look at that, you're getting all pink and flustered. Just confirms my theory – age just makes it richer and better. Seen yourself in the mirror lately? Blooming like a well-tended rose garden!'

'God, have I put on so much weight?' said Gayatri in sudden panic. 'I know I've put on a bit, but seriously, Abha, am I looking too bloated?'

'Relax, ben! Just a little rounding off in all the right places is all. I'm sure Vishy is quite happy with the results.'

'Ah, you're impossible! But you can't distract me so easily. I need to know about the man of the hour.'

Abha sighed and poured herself another cup in complete silence.

'I don't know for the life of me where it's headed, ben. Scares the living daylights out of me when I think about it, which isn't often. It started quite inauspiciously, with a quarrel over lunch in the presence of a third party. But things got sorted out over a couple of meetings and then whoosh, we soared into the blue sky yonder in an agony of ecstasy!'

Gayatri giggled. 'Enough, Abha. Stop bullshitting and give me the story. Also give me some more tea.'

Abha grinned and poured.

'Sorry, couldn't help the bullshit; I plough through reams of it every day and felt like quoting. Anyway, we met to discuss the manuscript of his first book that Preeti had sent me – she's a literary agent, the rising star I keep talking about. Now I've known Preeti for several years. She has a hawk eye and superb judgement, but when she said it was by a "senior political correspondent" of a major newspaper I thought, "Oh god, another semi-literate journo with exalted ideas about his knowledge of politics and an excessively casual attitude towards grammar." Then Preeti said it was a detective novel so I sent her an xoxo and promised to look at it soon. It kept lying around for a couple of weeks and I took it up one weekend when I finally had the time.'

'So you rejected it?' said Gayatri.

'God, no! I stayed up most of the night to finish it; it was really good! But there were some things that needed fixing, as always.' Abha pulled her tired-editor face. 'So I asked Preeti to bring the author along to the office for a meeting. And I promised them lunch.'

Abha lapsed into silence and it wasn't long before Gayatri protested.

'This is worse than a complicated surgery! Do I have to drag the story out of you piece by piece, Abha?'

Abha shook her head.

'No, you don't, ben. Sorry. Anyway, in came Preeti half an hour late with this tall, bulky man with grey in his hair, rumpled, bespectacled and rather intelligent-looking, sans khadi kurta and jhola, thank God. My first reaction was that he was rather sexy and bound to be much married and supremely arrogant and I got all my defences ready. And boy, did I need them. We discussed the book in detail and I had to get all my guards up so I wouldn't be distracted by his oh-so-seductive voice.'

'Yes, darling sister, his voice, his chin, his hair, his attitude, even his paunch, slight though it is,' teased Gayatri.

Abha laughed.

'Yes, yes, tease all you want, I kept my hormones on a tight leash and was all business. He figured I'd read the manuscript carefully and we had a pretty good conversation. He took my suggestions well – accepted some right away and agreed to brood on the rest and get back to me asap. Lunch was served and it was then that things turned exciting.'

'What did you do, poke fun at his hair or something?'

'Much worse. I passed a disapproving remark – although it was thoughtless and superficial – about his favourite poet! God, he really took me apart, gently but very firmly indeed, and halfway through I was not even listening – just thinking that I would like to pull him down to the floor and jump him right there!'

'You are impossible, Abha! You didn't do anything stupid, did you?'

'Relax, ben, I did nothing of the sort. Just continued fighting back till I was routed comprehensively and Preeti had to intervene to end the drama. Then they were on their way and I thought I'd never see him again.'

'But you did.'

'You bet. He called the next day and asked me out to dinner, the shameless man.'

'And you went too.'

'Of course I did. If he hadn't called, I was going to call him the next day anyway, with some silly excuse or other, but it wasn't needed, praise the lord!'

'And things took a turn I suppose? No more fights?'

'Well,' said Abha slowly and thoughtfully. 'You know, sometimes a spirited argument, even a fight, can be a good lead-up to a good you-know-what. Don't look so horrified, I didn't put out on the first date, no way!' Abha paused and grinned wickedly at her elder sister.

'I put out on the third. The second time was a play and I was on my period, or who knows what might've happened.'

Gayatri looked at her sister with gentle amusement.

'I think I know very well! Now, the gory details apart, what else keeps you together? Has to be something significant – I haven't seen you, um, going steady in this manner ever.'

'God, what an antediluvian expression, if ever there was one, ben! Interesting though, I haven't analyzed our relationship much, I'm just too busy feeling attracted to an incredible man.'

Abha was quiet for a long time, sipping her tea and staring at the drizzle. Gayatri was silent too, waiting.

Abha poured herself a final cup of tea.

'The one thing that really sets him apart is that he's an adult, whereas most men are children. They can be many things you know – attractive, intelligent, decent – I hate the word "nice" – considerate and what have you, but fundamentally, they remain children who want looking after. Don't you agree, ben?'

Gayatri nodded agreement – she didn't want to break her sister's train of thought.

'At the core, most men are babies. I'm not saying they don't have adult dimensions to their persona, many do – but still, at the core, they remain children. Mo, however, is mostly all grown up. He's also sexy, intelligent and enormously well read: he's read more Shakespeare than I have and everything from Plato to the Upanishads, plus he digs Rankin! You should see his library! I keep wondering why he's a bloody journalist and not a professor somewhere. Anyway, there you are, that's my Mo. And what are you looking at me like that for?'

Gayatri smiled. 'Waiting for you to finish.'

Abha took a deep breath. 'Big sisters are awful! Okay, Mo is a wonderful man, I have fallen head over fucking heels in love and I have no idea where it's heading and I don't care at this point. What I have is a sense of complete certainty and that's what I'm hanging on to.'

Gayatri smiled, happiness and relief on her face. 'At last, Abha, at long last! Don't shy away, just plunge in, my dear. And don't be afraid.'

Abha looked at her sister quizzically for a moment, then leaned across and hugged her.

The sisters sat quietly together as the rain clouds thundered, lightning flashed and the rain poured down.

'Gotta run, ben, too much bloody tea this morning. Have to wash my hair in this darned weather and then I'm out for the day, yesss!'

19

Sanju finished his MA exams and the family went on a European holiday. His parents were nominated for a two-week course at some German university and when that was over they went around Germany and bits of France by car. The chauffeur-driven vehicle was arranged by some 'friends' of his father, as were the hotels they stayed in.

'Guess what, Mummy! Sanju's having beer with his father on their Europe trip!' Akku yelled. 'He sent me photos of them, swigging from these huge mugs in a Bavarian beer house.'

'Imagine that,' replied Gayatri. 'A grown-up son drinking with his father in the presence of his mother, in public too.'

'You are so unfair,' Akku protested. 'They're quite conservative actually, but can't you see how they're changing as well? Sanju's parents are really nice to me when I go over to their house. Sanju and I hang out in his room and if they're at home, they never come in or anything.'

'Wonderful. That's good to know, my darling. But I've been meaning to ask you, Akku, do you have any long-term plans with Sanjay?'

'Wow, Mummy, after all these years seeing us together, you still need to ask? And if you must know, I plan to marry him and spend the rest of my life with him and the children we will have. No, I'm not like my friends who're busy playing the field – I've practically grown up with Sanju and can't even imagine myself with anyone else. And I'm financially independent already, like you've always wanted me to be, and soon he will be, too. I love him, Mummy, no doubts there at all. You don't have a problem, do you?'

Gayatri shook her head. 'No problem, child. Just one thing, I hope he feels the same way, and his parents, too.'

Akku got up and hugged Gayatri hard – an uncommon event between mother and daughter.

'Don't worry, Ma, of course he feels the same way – I've got it out of him on a number of occasions!

I can't say the same for his parents. They're nice, but somewhat cold and distant people, too. But they want their son to be happy, that's for sure. So chill! All the community and caste business doesn't matter to them either – they're an educated, modern family as far as I can tell. So worry not, Mummy. See how much I'm saving from my salary. I'll be a good Gujju housewife, I promise you – shining kitchen, the works!'

'All well and good, then,' said Gayatri. 'But whatever happened to your plans to do a PhD? I remember you said that you need one, that a BTech is just not enough to explore the possibilities of Computer Science …'

Akku considered this.

'I've thought about it, but for the moment it's not working out, Mummy. Hardly any serious work is happening in India in my area of interest, and going abroad does not fit in with my plans at the moment. Maybe a little way down the line … Anyway, I've got to put the final touches to a presentation for a major bid. Good break from writing Java code! Chalo, goodnight.'

Gayatri eventually went to bed. Vishy was out of town, Abha was out on the town, and she suddenly felt very troubled and lonely.

20

Rashmi and Rajiv Saran were both out of the country when the UPSC announced the Civil Services results. Sanjay Saran was placed twenty-fifth, a shoo-in for his service of choice – the Administrative Service. Both parents were, of course, keeping track and knew almost as soon as Sanjay did and both called him before he could call them. God was thanked, Sanju's hard work was praised and a Europe trip for the young man sanctioned by a delighted father who was completing a short lucrative assignment with the International Bank for Reconstruction and Development.

'My old friend from college, Ranjit Gupta, is posted in Paris and of course Bobby uncle is in Rome, so you can do both these great cities. Spend a week in each place – you'll find it a wonderful experience.

All you need is a very good pair of walking shoes! I'll speak to someone in Air India for your ticket. Make your plan for end June; both places will be jam-packed with tourists, but that's also part of the fun. And congratulations, once again, son. Hard work and commitment do get results after all.'

Rashmi Saran returned from her meetings in New York within a week and a round of temple visits and get-togethers with relatives followed, interspersed with visits to the malls and tailors for some dedicated wardrobe replenishment.

'We don't patronize French haute couture brands, Sanju, but that doesn't mean we dress shabbily either,' she clarified when Sanju protested at the number of suits she was ordering from the family tailor in Khan Market.

Akku was still busy at work, but their celebrations, before Sanju's parents returned, were both extensive and intense. Elaborate plans also got made.

'I'll catch the Friday night train to Dehradun every weekend and find a nice hotel near your Academy, take the Sunday night train back and head straight to work the next morning, toothbrush in hand!' Akku said.

'We'll see, Akku,' Sanju replied. 'God knows what the schedules are going to be like. I could be busy with this and that over the weekends; they say a lot of stuff happens during that time. Instead, why don't you join me on my Rome and Paris trip, or at least one of those cities?' He gave Akku a nudge. 'We'll find a cheap hotel for you – plenty on Trip Advisor – I'll slip out of whatever uncle's house I'll be staying at, and we'll get it on. Say what, Akriti Patel-Bansal?'

'You will be staying with various embassy 'uncles' and 'aunts' and I'll be rotting in some dingy BnB where you'll sneak in for a quickie every once in a while? Sounds like a plan, lover boy!' snapped Akku. 'Sorry boss! In any case I don't have leave or much money to waste. I'm saving it up for more important things.'

'Oh God, Akku, do you always have to be so irrational and negative about everything I say? Relax, yaar. And even if you're not coming, we still have to make up for lost time, so just get over here and let me teach you something new I read about the other day.'

'Now we're talking!' said Akku as the lesson began – she was very much in love indeed.

Soon Sanju went to Europe and had as much fun as he could amidst his embassy uncles and aunts, while

Akku continued working, saving and fantasizing about the future.

On his return, the features editor of a major daily got in touch with Sanju for an interview – they were doing a story on the career choices of students from 'elite' institutions as opposed to the slightly less fortunate.

'These second-rate hacks are absolutely bloody impossible!' Sanju fumed when the story finally came out. 'Apparently the best are now going to the IIMs and looking towards a career in business while only the substandard are opting for government. Agreed a lot more of the Hindi-medium-wallahs are now coming in, but the Service still gets the best there is around. If that wasn't the case, we would've gone to the dogs a long time ago.'

'But what does the data suggest?' asked Akku in all innocence and Sanju exploded.

'There's no fucking data at all. Just vague impressions and preconceived notions; ignorance compounded by arrogance! Drag everything down into the mud out of sheer bloody envy and frustration. And these are the defenders of democracy – God help us all.'

And suddenly it was time to leave for Mussoorie, home to the Academy that trained young bureaucrats in the art and science of governance. The Sarans decided to drive up to drop Sanju off and incidentally also meet up with a batchmate now posted at the Academy itself.

Akku and Sanju's goodbyes extended over several passionate encounters and took an enormous emotional toll. Tears were shed and commitments of eternal love made and reiterated.

'Let me settle down a bit, Akku, and we'll talk and fix up a weekend programme for you to come up,' was Sanju's parting gift before getting into the car with his parents and driving off one early morning to begin what he felt was going to be a brave new chapter in his life.

21

From: Akriti Bansal <akkuthepatel@abcmail.com>
To: Sanjay Saran <imsanjaysaran@gomail.com>

Sanju my love,

It's been so lonely since you went off. I'm working crazy hours to stay sane, or I get seriously upset, babe. And I can't even drink like you boys to drown my sorrows; you know I either fall asleep or start puking, so I've quit trying (and you better not start laughing). Please write a long mail, na, not the two-line scrawls you deign to send every few days.

They tell me the matchmaking starts as soon as the course begins at the Academy – say it isn't so, Sanju babu! A colleague's cousin was up there last year and told him that you optimize across community and cadre and pick a mate before the two-month foundation course is over and get married so that the two-year training programme becomes an officially sponsored honeymoon! You better keep your eyes off the ladies, lover boy! I'm planning to come over the last weekend of the month just to make sure; find a nice hotel for me, will you? I'll try and take Friday off and catch the morning Shatabdi.

Better get cracking on the long reply! I miss you more than I can say.

Love you,

Akku

⁓

From: Sanjay Saran <imsanjaysaran@gomail.com>
To: Akriti Bansal <akkuthepatel@abcmail.com>

Darling Akku,

Your friends and their worthy cousins are talking rubbish, take it from me. You can't tar everybody here with the same stereotypical brush, that's not really fair. Which is not to say there is no matchmaking going on, but that's only natural given the circumstances, and sort of makes sense, too, in a society where romantic love is more or less taboo and arranged marriages are the norm. If more attributes match, it's better than if only a few do, isn't it?

Oh, and don't get mad now, Akku, but your weekend plans will have to be postponed. My parents are driving up; some blasted family-type gatherings have been planned. Let's look at next month? I'll check the calendar and we'll fix something. Got to go – there's a debate coming up and I don't want to miss it – these things are so important.

Miss you, babe.

Bye,

Sanju

~

My dear Sanjay,

You are, I am sure, aware just how unhappy your mother and I are about your behaviour over the weekend.

Although we haven't been in touch for some years now, Mr and Mrs Verma are old family friends and their daughter a brilliant and beautiful girl, and so well behaved. Quite unlike you, I am sorry to say.

It is simply not appropriate that you spend the weekend with your nose buried in a book instead of talking and being social as is expected on such occasions. What we did not appreciate at all were your references to your friend Akriti in your conversation with Mrs Verma.

We have given you the utmost freedom while you were growing up and have never objected to your friendship with Akriti – a very decent and intelligent girl, I am sure. However, childhood friendships are best confined to childhood and you are past that stage now. You are an adult in one of the most demanding and fulfilling of occupations and you have to shoulder the responsibilities that come with your position – responsibilities to yourself, your family and your community. We do not exist in isolation. Life is lived within structures, otherwise there is chaos. The structures we have built over the years and are part of are solid. They support us, and we, in turn, owe them our loyalty. Family, of course, comes first, and family is embedded in community – and we belong to a highly regarded and proud community, as you are well aware. I have no doubt about your commitment to all that we hold dear, but I felt it my duty to remind you, now that you are stepping out into life where the laws of the jungle prevail and only the fittest survive. I'm afraid the carefree years of childhood and youth are over now, son. You have entered the real world.

You have two years of training to undergo and there is no hurry to settle down, but it is indeed time to consider your options, sooner rather than later, to decide upon a suitable partner for yourself.

We will never dictate your choice to you – that is not our way. We will, however, do our duty and make sure that you meet the most suitable young women that our community has to offer – the rest is up to you. I am already overwhelmed with proposals. Your mother and I are carefully considering them all and will select only the best for your consideration. You will agree that we have your best interests at heart and considerable experience and knowledge of the world.

There is, as I said, no hurry and absolutely no compulsion, but the process has to start now – these things take time. And, of course, you must move beyond your youthful friendships. Please remember, the best families tend to look askance at any hint of relationships beyond the common casual friendships of childhood. So, please, now politely but firmly end the connection with Dr Bansal's daughter. They are good people, I am sure, but not our people.

I am sure you will give serious consideration to what I have said. I look forward to hearing from you soon.

Vijay Bahadur Mathur, our ambassador to the US and an old and dear friend, will be visiting next month with family and we plan to drive up one weekend, so keep your calendar clear.

Regards,

Papa

~

A month went by and Sanju took to walking to Mall Road every evening and slowly making his way through three or four large drinks – Old Monk and Coke it was, the best return for money – and restlessly walking back for dinner. Sleep didn't come easy; his mind was preoccupied but he couldn't quite tell with what. The training curriculum was not especially challenging, so his performance remained unaffected. Socially, he had always been quiet and withdrawn, so to all appearances things seemed as good as ever for Master Sanjay Saran.

~

My dear Nana,

I'm in an impossible situation. There are only wrong answers to every question I ask myself and there is no one to turn to either. You know what

Ma and Papa are like – good people but with clear and rigid views. I could spend my life very happily with Akku, as she's expecting me to, but my parents will be completely devastated if I go down that road. For them, it is simply not acceptable and after Papa's letter I just cannot bring myself to even raise the issue with them. It will hurt them enormously, all their dreams and ambitions for me, their standing amongst their peer group, basically the community to which they so proudly belong. Everything they've worked and lived and sacrificed for will turn to dust and ashes. I'm their only child, the sole focus of their attentions, God help me! I agree with Papa that I've lived in a rather confined world, socially and emotionally – Akku and I have known each other since we were in kindergarten! And maybe, just maybe, it is time to step into the real world outside, which I do realize is much bigger than I had thought. But does that mean dropping Akku from my life altogether? Perhaps relationships from one's youth do indeed have an expiry date and growing up means moving on beyond them. God, how terrible that sounds! But the more I think about it, the more I realize that I have a life to live in a particular socio-cultural milieu, a relatively traditional and conservative context, while she is a child of the new world, of software systems and Californian sunshine, and I'm bound for the dusty villages of Bihar in all likelihood – how can this ever work? I don't know, Nana, I just don't know what to do. And you never reply to me anyway. I've never felt so alone Nana, never!

Sanju

~

Over the next few months, the Sarans drove up twice with 'old friends' who just happened to have young, beautiful, accomplished daughters of marriageable age, and Sanju, still seriously conflicted, stayed polite but non-committal.

~

Dear Nana,

I must admit Mummy and Papa have been true to their word – not a hint of pressure to say yes to any of the 'eligibles' they have been parading over the last few months. But I can see that they honestly cannot think of a bahu outside the community – it's a nightmare they cannot handle. I can't imagine being the source of so much anxiety and tension to the people I love so much. And why must the whole notion of love be so damned complex and contradictory and hurtful anyway? It's supposed to be wonderful, right? All bullshit. Life is not about love at all, at least not the romantic love I fantasized about. And all is not for the best in this best of all fucking possible worlds. No, Nana, not at all.

And by the way, I've underplayed it with Akku, but the dating game is in full swing here. Most of the uncommitted ladies are rather friendly, some a good deal more friendly than others, I tell you. This, of course, is constrained by Community and Service, though the constraint isn't altogether difficult to overcome; 'upward mobility' is generally permissible! It's natural, Nana – these are the young men and women who will run this country in the near future and dating within a close-knit community is always safer. I must also add that dating here is most often, though not always, linked to matrimony. There's been a lot of fun and games, which is inevitable with so many of us thrown together in class, on treks, village visits, group presentations and what have you, but the danger that a few snogging sessions will be followed by an introduction to Mummy and Daddy coincidentally up for a visit is rather high! So restraint is a safer option here, as painful as it may be!

But all this apart, Nana, I still don't know what to do about this whole Akku business. And there is no one I can ask, either.

Sanju

~

One Saturday evening, as he was walking back from the Mall, troubled and inebriated, it finally dawned on him that he could procrastinate no more. It was time to take a call. It was all so overwhelming that he stumbled a little and then sat down on the pavement for a while. 'The wisdom to know what you cannot change is the highest wisdom,' he muttered to himself a trifle unsteadily and slumped, his head in his hands. When he heard voices coming towards him from the direction of town, he got up hurriedly and resumed his stroll back to the Academy.

Sanju woke up late the next day. By eleven, however, he had got his first draft ready and by lunchtime, the email was ready to be sent. He stared at the words on the screen for a brief second and hit Send, turned and left the room.

22

Dinner over, the dishes done, Abha and Mo sat in the enclosed veranda of Abha's little mountain cottage and looked out at the valley below, defined after sunset by the twinkling lights scattered here and there.

'What's got you down, Abby?' said Mo, when the silence had gone on for too long. 'Swimming in deep emotional waters or is it just gas from the chana-bhatura?'

Abha smiled and punched him on the shoulder. 'I don't know what it is, but something's making me feel very low today.'

'I didn't bring this on, did I?' said Mo. 'I know I had my column to finish *and* had a headache coming on so ignored your not-so-subtle invitations.'

Abha laughed and threw a cushion at him. 'Stop it, I don't want to be amused. I want to glower at the world and be glum and insecure and frightened and I want a large brandy, if you will be so kind.'

'Sure,' said Mo and got up to fetch the cognac and glasses from the kitchen, ruffling her hair as he passed her.

'Don't do that,' Abha snapped. 'You know I don't like it!'

Mo smiled to himself, came back with the fixings and handed her a glass.

'The only ways out of depression are lust or anger and it's a bit too early after dinner for the former, darling. So, I'm doing my best to provoke you to anger. Simple.'

'Don't, please, please don't,' muttered Abha and buried her head in her hands.

'Oh shit,' said Mo as he finished his drink in one swallow and moved over to put his arms around Abha and pull her close to him. 'Abby dearest, what's the matter with you? We had a great day, a glorious meal to round it off and Remy Martin to follow! And me beside you, not singing in the wilderness! What more do you need for Paradise?'

'Nothing, but you probably want a nice, good girl, don't you? All men do. And that, as you know, I am not, by any stretch of the imagination,' said Abha in a choked voice.

Mo was taken aback but kept his composure. 'And where exactly are you going with this? Also, hey, hey, take this tissue please, don't drip snot down my favourite kurta!'

Abha accepted the tissue, blew her nose and stuffed it into the pocket of Mo's kurta.

'I was so happy and content all day, thinking how lucky and I am and that's when suddenly my whole life came up before my eyes. It was so terrible, Mo! I suppose it's true – I've been a promiscuous, alcoholic bitch since bloody puberty and when you realize that you'll just leave me and go away and I'll be all alone again. I've been lonely most of my life, you know, always the outsider and now I finally have something real and you'll go away, too. And I'll be back to where I always was, except this time I'll just be an old and bitter hag.'

Mo took a deep breath.

'First of all, my dear, you have to shift a little – my arm is totally numb from your not-too-inconsiderable weight resting on it.' He gently moved Abha, released his long-suffering arm and sighed.

'All this is your damn missionary school education resurfacing. Sin, guilt and absolution become your defining elements if you're around priests and nuns for too long – this is personal experience speaking. And I've spent many years sinning carefully and comprehensively to work it all out of my system!'

Mo paused, took firm hold of Abha's hands and continued.

'So, first of all, by the powers vested in me by the Lord of Common Sense and Humanity, I absolve you of all sins of omission and commission you may have committed in the past, present and future. Amen. And that will be a thousand rupees, thank you.'

Abha sniffed and giggled at the same time and Mo tightened his grip on her hands.

'Okay, now in all seriousness,' he said, 'I love you, Abha Patel, and will, inshallah, do so for the rest of my life. Anything you want me to add to this? No? And this is despite you having lived only a mildly adventurous life till you met me. Ever since, it's become seriously hot, but no blame attaches to you for that – the fault is all mine. Okay, all done. Now smile please, thank you.'

Abha laughed.

'Remember, darling ji,' Mo continued, 'the only trouble with, umm, shall we say sexual adventure, is the potential for unmentionable diseases, and in that respect, both of us are free and clear. Your liver, too, if I remember your medical report right, is working away just fine. So let's not call you an alcoholic just yet. And don't even ask about *my* liver.'

Abha sat up straight. 'What was that? I never even saw your blood test report. You told me it was all fine and the report was misplaced! Tell me, Mo, there's nothing wrong, is there?'

Mo laughed. 'Ah ha, I knew that would get you listening! Nothing to worry about, my love; the SGOT/SGPT values are at the upper end of normal, that's all. Why do you think I've shifted to wine and exercise from whiskey and indolence? Okay, your turn to talk – my throat's hurting. Haven't done so much yammering in years.'

Abha slowly leaned forward and kissed Mo, first gently then with increasing vehemence.

'So you won't just leave me one fine day and walk off into the sunset, will you?' said Abha when they finally drew apart.

Mo shook his head. 'Till death do us part. And even then I'll be waiting just across the divide and we'll take up from where we left off right away!'

'Good. Gimme some more of this good stuff then.'

Mo complied and they sat quietly together for a very long time, drinking and staring out into the night.

Then Abha stirred and asked softly, 'What did you say were the two paths out of depression, Mo?'

Mo smiled but remained silent.

'Ah well, if you don't remember, all I can say is I'm done with anger for now, so ...' She paused, Mo smiled broadly, stood and picked her up in his arms.

'Your wish is my command, ma'am,' he said gently. 'Now and for evermore.'

23

From: Sanjay Saran <imsanjaysaran@gomail.com>
To: Akriti Bansal <akkuthepatel@abcmail.com>

My dear Akku,

I am writing to you after a very long period of serious reflection. I have been troubled, agonized even, by the changes that have happened in my life over the past few months and getting my head around them has been painful to say the least.

I realize now that a major transition has occurred and one must review one's life and plans for the future in the context of this change.

We must come to terms with the fact that the carefree days of childhood and youth are over and one has now entered a new adult world, which is far less comfortable and more demanding than the earlier one. We can no longer afford to indulge ourselves in what we alone want – there are other demands on us – serious demands that require serious consideration. We have been together since kindergarten – years of enormous joy and friendship. But we've also been in a little bubble together, just us, for so long we forgot that there is another world outside, the real world, one can say. And the uncomfortable realities of this world have burst the bubble and I'm now adjusting to the new context – it has taken me time; it's been an intensely painful struggle.

I have, however, come to some serious conclusions. Life has brought to an end our time together, Akku. Yes, painful as the thought is, it is true and denying it is simply hiding one's head in the sand; childish escape is no longer permitted, I'm afraid.

You are young and part of a brave new world: software systems, California, artificial intelligence and neural networks – the cutting edge of science and the passport to success. I, on the other hand, am sinking into a world still populated by patwaris, gram pradhans, criminal politicians and open defecation. The two can interface, of course, and I fully intend to implement the emerging notions of e-governance in whichever field and geography I am posted to; but my world is fundamentally different now, more conservative and old-fashioned than I had ever thought. My parents, to whom you know I owe everything, want a certain future for me that is in keeping with their notions of what is right and good and it would be enormously selfish and self-centred of me to insist on following my own path, or at least what appeared to be the right path till very recently. I cannot, in any conscience, cause my parents the agony that will surely result from us maintaining our relationship instead of me settling down in the manner they consider correct and appropriate. What I'm saying is that our relationship must now end, Akku. It's terribly painful but there is no option, none at all.

I know this will hurt you and it hurts me too, enormously, but it is the right thing to do. You will get over me soon, I know, and build a happy and successful life for yourself.

Parting will lead to sorrow no doubt, but in our case, it is inevitable.

I wish you all the very best for the future.

Regards,

Sanjay

When her laptop pinged, announcing a mail, Akku tossed aside the clothes she was folding and jumped to open it. Sanju had not replied to her mails for almost two weeks and not taken her calls either and she was feeling increasingly uneasy. She clicked open the mail and read it with growing disbelief, then read it a second time, very slowly. Her heart was pounding, and there was a strange roaring in her ears. Was this some kind of joke that Sanju was playing? But he had never been given to pranks. She picked up her mobile and called him. The phone rang and rang and rang. 'He's in the loo,' she told herself and called again and again and again.

And then suddenly he answered.

'Sanju, baby, I just got your mail – what kind of joke was that? It's a joke, right? Tell me honestly … you're giving me such a scare …'

'It's no joke, Akku. We have to grow up and face the real world,' interrupted Sanju abruptly.

'Our world *is* the real world, Sanju! How can you say that all these years suddenly don't matter? What's going on, Sanju? What's really happened?'

'I've said all I had to say in my mail and it's final, Akku. I'm sorry but it's for the best. You take care, bye.'

Sanju disconnected, pulled on a jacket and walked to town. He needed a drink.

Akku stared at her phone in a daze, then hit redial. The phone rang for a minute before cutting off.

Akku sat in a daze for a while, picked up her laptop, walked across to the living room where her mother and aunt were chatting, and wordlessly handed the computer to Abha.

'Akku, what's the matter?' said Gayatri, holding out her arms as she saw her daughter's stricken face. Akku knelt at her mother's feet and put her head in her lap. Gayatri gently stroked her thick unruly hair, and that's when the tears came.

~

From: Abha Patel <abhaedits@abcmail.com>
To: Gayatri Bansal <gpbansal@mailer.com>

Dear ben,

I think we did the right thing in bringing Akku here. The weather is beautiful – cold but sunny, and the silence seems to be seeping into us all. We walk for an hour every morning, either chatting or in silence, as the mood strikes us, and I, for one, am exhausted by the end of it.

I sit with tea and biscuits afterwards – the paper comes late – while Akku goes to a tai-chi class that an elderly Finnish couple run just down the road. She was in their diplomatic service; India was her last posting before she retired, and he is a writer and editor. They moved here three years ago.

Before you ask, yes, your daughter's eating reasonably well, if not heartily, and no longer losing weight. Breakfast and lunch are my responsibility, since in two weeks' time Akku will have to get it together and start leaving for work before me. We cook dinner together; she's picked up so many tricks in Cali!

In this whole fucking mess this was an unexpected bonus – the ease with which they agreed to three weeks' leave and for her to work from home for two weeks after that. Akku, of course, tells me it's only because she is between two big projects and there really isn't too much for her to do right now.

She's a strong girl, your daughter. The support you and Vishy have given her and whatever I have contributed seems to have had some effect; she's come out of denial and from the looks of it, the self-pity will soon be out the window. She's growing up, our little girl. Only wish it wasn't so hard, so soon.

I've adopted a puppy – a cute thing I call Bhutia; he's already big and plump after all the pampering he's got from Akku and me. We went down to Haldwani to introduce him to his vet and get him his first set of shots. Akku's claimed responsibility of our newest family member and he keeps her rather busy cleaning up after him!

It breaks my heart to see her like this, but I feel she's beginning to surface. That first week had frightened the shit out of me, but now I'm feeling a little reassured.

We're going to start making dinner now – tonight it's a la Julia Child – we're doing sautéed chicken with mushrooms in a white wine sauce. Getting quite gourmet here, wouldn't you say?

Look forward to seeing you and Vishy next week – don't forget to get the booze and the cold meats. The cold bag works well enough; just pack enough ice in it.

Love,
Abha

From: Abha Patel <abhaedits@abcmail.com>
To: Gayatri Bansal <gpbansal@mailer.com>

My dear ben,

It was great having the two of you up here. The effect on Akku has been significant and I'm slowly beginning to unclench my teeth and breathe easy. I still wake up in the night to check on her, but I think the worst may just be over.

I'm not sure what you and Vishy said to her on your long walks together, but I see her making a major effort to pull herself together. The most encouraging sign is that she's responded to my gentle prodding about the PhD. It'll be amazing if that works out – she'll get away from here and stay involved in something that she both loves and is good at. God damn that lousy bastard's soul to hell!

Now the fucking dog has pooped on my carpet again.

In haste,

Abha

~

From: Gayatri Bansal <gpbansal@mailer.com>
To: Abha Patel <abhaedits@abcmail.com>

My dear Abha,

Your instincts are probably right – they usually are and I trust them. It was all Vishy's doing, believe me. I gave Akku my 'tough love' as you call it, but towards the end, after Vishy had spent hours chatting about God knows what – Himalayan ecology, American politics, AI and other sundries – I just lost track. But he always drew her out, got her talking and getting herself out of her misery and acknowledging that the world is larger and still interesting, and exciting. We had very long silences on our long walks too, I assure you. I just watched her slowly peer out of the dark well she's in and, when I thought she was ready, gave her a bit – a very little bit – of tough love. I told her she had no monopoly on heartbreak and misery, that shit happens to everyone in different ways and our strength lies in how well we deal with it. I think in the end she took it rather well. If only the 'why-me-poor-me' can be taken care of, a bit of pure grief might just be healthy and shouldn't last too long, I hope. Anyway, keep me posted and we'll see if we can come up again next weekend.

Love,
Gayatri

24

From: Akriti Bansal <akkuthepatel@abcmail.com>
Top: Gayatri Bansal <gpbansal@mailer.com>

Dear Mummy,

You all can start breathing easy now – I'm on the mend. Thanks to Vishy uncle, you and Abha Maasi, I am now efficiently functional, I think. Work pressure's building up too – I'll be playing a major role in a big upcoming project.

I've been thinking seriously about applying for a PhD and have even started filling applications and chasing up references – how's that for getting better? The recommendations should be in by early December, which doesn't give me much time, but I'll manage.

As you said, 'shit happens' and what matters is how one deals with it and I'm doing my best.

Maasi tells me you're driving up and that we'll go home together. Looking forward to that, Mummy! There's a new place in Haldwani that sells the most delicious samosas ever – we have to stop there for breakfast!

Love,

Akku

~

Abha and Akku were on the return leg of their morning walk when Akku broke the silence for the first time.

'You know, Maasi, I think I've lost the capacity for love now. I mean romantic love. I did a mental exercise last night; I tried to imagine myself in a romantic situation – sexual-romantic – and I almost puked! Honestly, I can't think of a man in physical terms any more, or emotional either. The thought makes me sick! No, no, I'm not going to become some sort of nun. I'm a software engineer and I hope to become a seriously good and highly qualified one in due course, but for now that's about it and that's a little depressing.'

Abha suppressed a smile and said, 'Well, as the family expert on human relationships, all I can say is that this takes time to heal, so give it some time, Akku dearest. A serious relationship has deep roots and when uprooted so suddenly it leaves a wound that takes time to heal.'

Abha regarded her own words for a minute; she knew it was time for tough love.

'Okay, fuck it, I don't want to bullshit my baby, so please listen to me when I tell you that life does provide a strong healing functionality along with the usual kicks up the butt. It takes time, and you of all people should understand the need for and value of process. You have to acknowledge the hurt, experience it, grieve for what you have lost and only then can you possibly begin to heal. So don't theorize about life, just live it and see how it evolves and deal with it as best you can. Life does not change, but you must, so you can grow to deal with it. And you are doing so. I've seen it in the last month. Just keep at it with all the buddhi you can muster. Now enough psychobabble; what say we make pancakes and scrambled eggs for breakfast and coq au vin for dinner? Let's not forget about the wine either! Remember we have to finish all the booze and food before we leave in four days. My "work-from-home" bonanza ends soon and who knows when I can come up here again?'

Akku was very quiet all day. Dinner involved a reasonably successful coq au vin and a fair amount of wine, after which she turned to Abha and said, 'Have you ever actually experienced this sort of rejection and betrayal, Maasi? Tell me to shut up and I will, but from all your advice on how to deal with the kicks I thought maybe ...'

Abha took a deep breath, a quick decision and a large gulp of wine for support.

'Yes, my dear, I have. Which is why I'm not giving you any gyan out of some *Book for Broken Hearts* that makes my company so much money. But I still need alcohol to talk about it, so hand me that bottle. And no more for you, your mother will kill me if I help you turn alcoholic!'

Abha poured herself a glass and firmly put the cap back on the bottle.

'A long time ago, in a galaxy far, far away,' she intoned in a deep dramatic voice and laughed. Akku giggled and Abha nodded agreement. 'Yes, let's not take ourselves too seriously here, okay? So, as I was saying, once upon a time, when I was young and susceptible to a handsome face, a gentle smile, a brilliant mind, I fell in love: totally, absolutely and completely, with every fibre of my being.'

She took a sip, put her glass down and looked across at her niece – young, vulnerable, hurting.

'Jokes apart, Akku, he was my everything.

'He was my North, my South, my East and West,

My working week and my Sunday rest...

You can giggle all you want, but he got it so right, Auden did!

I had slogged during my undergrad days but I also played the field with abandon. So, on one of my nights out I met this guy in a pub. A couple of friends and I were getting quite smashed, when I was introduced to this group of guys doing much the same thing. The Brits really drink a lot, particularly the young ones. Anyway, this man seemed quiet, pleasant, intelligent and the most sober of the whole bunch. We met again by design the next day and the next and so on. Without going into the gory details, we moved in together within a month and spent three years happily in love. In my last year, I was putting the finishing touches to my thesis, when one day I felt a little sick in the library and came home very early to find him in bed with a sexy young undergrad!'

Abha paused, took a deep breath, then continued. 'Prosaic and straight out of a third-rate movie, huh? But life can be a damn sight stranger, more than any movie yet made. To cut a long story short, I was quite a mess for a while, though I made sure it was only a short while because I had a thesis to submit and no horny, unfaithful son of a bitch was going to deprive me of that. I submitted by the deadline and went for a long walking tour in the Scottish wilds, eating a little, drinking a lot and feeling very sorry for myself. When that was over, I was beginning to run out of money, and that's when I got a job offer in publishing in London – I had interviewed with a number of houses and had nearly given up hope when this place called. I jumped at it. Six months later, they asked me to move back to India as they were setting up shop here and so I arrived just in time to take you to kindergarten.'

Abha drained her glass and both aunt and niece looked out at the moonlight flooding the valley below Abha's cottage, high up on Crank's Ridge.

25

THE GRANDDAUGHTER OF RAI BAHADUR SURYA KANT Verma and daughter of India's ambassador to the United Nations, Shri Mahesh Kumar Mathur and his good wife Smt Susheela Mathur, had a BA (Hons) degree in English Literature from Lady Shri Ram College and had trained in Kuchipudi and Hindustani classical vocals from the age of five.

At twenty years of age, soon after starting her MA, her guru approved her arangetram, which was, of course, held at the India International Centre, and friends, extended family and those who matter in Lutyens' Delhi were invited. Among the invitees were Mrs Rashmi and Mr Rajiv Saran and their son Sanjay, home on a short vacation before beginning the more 'advanced' elements of Civil Services training.

As expected, young Sarala Mathur delivered an outstanding performance. She had worked very hard, looked absolutely stunning and the bhava which she projected was unexpectedly powerful in one so young.

Sarala's parents hosted a dinner after the performance in the private dining room of the Centre and the Sarans were amongst the invitees. Sanjay and Sarala were introduced and soon got into an animated conversation that ranged from the relevance of temple-based art forms in modern secular life to the poetry of Pablo Neruda.

The engagement ceremony was held in end March, after the young people had met several times and on two occasions had even gone out for dinner unescorted. Although Sanjay had to finish his training and Sarala her MA, it was decided that the wedding wouldn't be delayed overmuch and, within fifteen months of joining the Service, Sanjay was wedded to Sarala Mathur – a major event in the social calendar of the residents of Lutyens' Delhi. Several Cabinet ministers attended and the PM himself sent an enormous bouquet with his regrets as he was travelling abroad.

Dear Nana

Here I am, safely shackled and not yet twenty-five. It's good to see Mummy and Papa so thrilled.

She's a very nice girl, Nana – intelligent, seriously gifted, beautiful and for a highly protected bade ghar ki badi beti from a rather orthodox family, reasonably forthcoming in bed after some gentle persuasion. It's amazing – shringaar ras is fine on stage in a public performance, but inhibitions take over when you get their clothes off in private. She's ambitious too, which is all to the good – can't expect women today to be happy simply keeping house and playing good wife and mother. Traditionally though, one is either a classical dancer or a classical singer, but she intends to be both. I'm not sure if it will work out; her plans will require her to spend a great deal of time in Delhi at her parents' place, but you could say that's part of the deal. Anyway, for the moment, all's for the best in this best of all possible worlds, the Maldives is beautiful and the dreary real world is far, far away.

Sanju

~

Akriti was admitted to the graduate programme of the Computer Science department at Stanford University;

classes were to begin in the fall. She left for California in August, a few months before Sanju's wedding. Her mother and Vishy accompanied her to help her settle in and then have a short, much-overdue holiday of their own in Sonoma Valley. Abha went over for the Christmas break, took Akku out on a driving trip up the coast to Seattle and returned very relieved at Akku's return to near normalcy.

'She'll be okay, ben,' Abha reported on her return. 'She hasn't started dating yet – says she's too busy with her work. We need to give her time. She's done very well in all her courses and another successful semester will establish her firmly in the academic sphere. With that confidence, who knows, she might finally take the leap. For now, I feel her focus on work is the right thing; everything else can wait.'

Gayatri nodded agreement, she understood well enough the value of time and hard professional work as healers.

26

Akku did not come home during the summer break after her first year – she got a summer internship instead. She did, however, take a brief holiday with her two apartment mates. They rented a car and drove to Grand Canyon, stopping at Las Vegas en route, where she won five hundred dollars on the slot machines.

The photos she sent home featured Amy Chen, the studious physicist from southern California, and Agnes Macintosh from Scotland, a mathematician in the final stretch of a difficult PhD programme.

～

From: Akriti Bansal <akkuthepatel@abcmail.com>
To: Abha Patel <abhaedits@abcmail.com>

Dear Maasi,

Year two begins. I have to finish a bunch of coursework this year to maintain my formal status in the department, so there's loads to do. Remember I had started tai-chi with that old Finnish couple in Almora? Well, I've resumed that here; there are classes held in the park across the road from our apartment block and I'm totally hooked. Our teachers, a middle-aged Chinese couple, are seriously qualified practitioners, Amy tells me, and it shows! Agnes hopes to finish this year – it'll be her sixth year in the programme and she's beginning to unravel a little. It's frightening, I tell you. My target is five: three years of coursework and two years of writing the dissertation; although in my field it might come to publishing a certain number of papers. Let's see how things go. And no, my darling Maasi, I have neither the time nor the emotional inclination to start dating. The thought no longer repels me so you can call it progress, but I'm too afraid – I can't handle another rejection – the thought is unbearable right now. Instead, I'm quite happy to be busy with classes; I go running twice a week and do tai-chi the rest of the days. It's a pretty good life. Agnes and I are going to Amy's place for Thanksgiving. You better come over for Christmas, Maasi. Do try.

Love,

Akku

Abha landed in San Francisco three days after the second academic year closed very satisfactorily for Akriti. She had completed the required coursework with excellent grades and was ready for a holiday before taking up a rather lucrative summer assignment. Abha rented a car and they drove around Southern California at a relaxed pace following a terrific itinerary that Amy had chalked out for them.

'Ten days of bliss!' said Akku as they returned to her apartment on Friday evening. 'Thank you so much, Maasi, for this and for everything else. Can't believe I have class on Monday. Aarrgh!'

'You are most welcome, my darling girl,' said Abha. 'I'll rest up today and then I'll start cooking – the next two days will be one long party. I'll go shopping tomorrow morning and we'll do biryani and beer; chicken curry and parathas the day after.'

'Maasi, don't forget to make a gigantic pile of theplas for my fridge! And then Monday you'll be off, oh God,' Akku said and hugged her aunt long and hard.

The third year was another slog redeemed only by Gayatri and Vishy's winter visit. They took Akriti to New York and everyone had a very good time, what with Broadway musicals, jazz clubs and the top-notch museums. The year ended well – Agnes finally submitted her dissertation with her guide's blessings and Akku, her thesis proposal, which was accepted by the committee.

'Now's the real test, Maasi,' wrote Akku. 'I've done the hard work, but can I add something new to the body of knowledge in my field or do I simply remain a good software engineer? Two years, that's it. If I can't do it in that time, I'm going back to a job that will make me a shitload of money! And we have a domestic problem, too. Agnes has finally submitted and will be leaving soon. She has a job offer back home in Edinburgh, and we need a new apartment mate in two weeks! The word's out – let's see what we get.'

What they got soon after Agnes left in a haze of alcohol and tears, was young Luke Walker, doomed, forever, to be called Sky by everyone and their grandmother.

'Yes, Maasi, we got someone just in time. He's a very nice guy, a six-footer, built like a barn, and … umm … a self-proclaimed redneck from Ohio – or is it Oklahoma – who claims he is the runt in a clan whose sole preoccupation is huntin', fishin' and drinkin' pissy 'merican beer and drivin' their trucks all over town looking for fights in bars! Before you get everything in a twist, Luke is a soft-spoken, highly regarded PhD candidate in the Department of East Asian Languages – I didn't even know there was such a department in the university – working on some aspect of medieval Chinese literature, and believe it or not, learning Sanskrit in his free time. He has a wicked sense of humour, too, and I suspect the clan he talks about is probably all artists or classical musicians or something like that in New England or some such! Anyway, we've all been exploring the nightlife here together. Nothing like a giant escorting you to make two small Asian women feel secure!

We've all become very good friends. And guess what? He's even invited us home for Thanksgiving! Imagine a tribe of tobacco-chewin', rifle-shootin' rednecks to go clubbing with (still hoping he's not playing the fool about that), if they have clubs in the heartland that is!

Anyway, I better wind up now. I'm trying to get my first paper done before Christmas, and if that's accepted, I'll be on my way! Bye Maasi, and please try to come over in the winter. We'll all go to Vegas and partyyy!

Give my love to Mo.'

From: Akriti Bansal <akkuthepatel@abcmail.com>
To: Abha Patel <abhaedits@abcmail.com>

Dear Maasi,

Thanksgiving was something else indeed. We went down to Iowa, the corn and soybean belt, to a zillion-acre farm run by Luke's father – a six-foot-five native Iowan. But there the stereotype collapses. John, the dad, was a professor of French for crying out loud! After graduating with a degree in French, he went to the Sorbonne on a scholarship and came back after five years with an advanced degree, a highly regarded book on some aspect of modern French literature and a five-foot-three wife from Bordeaux, as haute petite as they come. He taught for twenty-five years at the U of Iowa and then came to run the farm on his father's death. They have three children, two daughters and Luke, who is indeed not the runt of the family – his sisters are both like their mother in the looks department – small and beautifully French and hard-driving American otherwise; one is a hedge fund manager in New York and the other a doctor in the US Army, who's done two tours of duty in Afghanistan!

It was a fantastic weekend – genuinely nice and friendly company, great food and superb wines. And they have more books than even you, Abha Maasi!

Got to get back to work now. Bye.

Akku

27

Sanjay and Sarala Saran were blessed with twin daughters two years after marriage and Sarala subsequently went into a deep depression – she had wanted a son, as had everyone else who mattered, father, mother, father in-law, mother-in-law and last but not least, a tough old biddy of a grandmother. Sanju was the only one who found this incomprehensible.

~

My dear Nana,

I am stupefied. I have the most beautiful twin daughters and nobody but me seems to be thrilled about it! Of course, everyone is putting on a brave face and I've even been told – by my worthy mother of all people, the icon of women's independence and liberation – that after all, we are young and 'next time' will work out well! Jesus Christ

Almighty God and all the angels that can dance on the head of a pin! I don't know whether to laugh or to hit someone, starting with my beloved mother. Forgive me, Nana.

And as for my wife, she seems to think my happiness is contrived and hides a major disappointment. She's already apologized a dozen times and gets tearful at every opportunity. And here I thought that modern women understood the basic facts of human biology. I really and honestly cannot understand this and I am in a minority of one. I need a large drink or three to handle this, Nana, so bye for now.

Sanju

~

Sanju categorically refused to 'try' for another child. 'The world is overpopulated already,' he informed his wife when she hesitantly made the suggestion after the twins turned a year old, and their life settled on an even keel – stable, sensible and a trifle loveless. Sarala returned to her singing and spent increasingly more time in Delhi with her parents, while Sanju went through the purgatory of a series of Bihar postings. He soon acquired a reputation as a very hard-working, hands-on and results-oriented officer, quite different from the distant sahibs who generally graced the offices of state. He also began drinking rather heavily. There were occasional rumours about serial relationships with young, single lady officers and a more enduring one about a longish liaison with a very successful and highly regarded colleague who had gone through a messy divorce, but had remained in the field doing very commendable development work. The general consensus was, however, that such rumours were inevitable about young men living alone in close proximity to youthful, unattached, independent, professional women and were usually baseless and best disregarded.

28

From: Akriti Bansal <akkuthepatel@abcmail.com>
To: Abha Patel <abhaedits@abcmail.com>

My dear Maasi,

I have news for you, great news, which is why this mail. My first paper has been forwarded to one of the leading publications in the field by my supervisory committee, and my guide, the great guru, has personally called up the editor and recommended it!

Three and a half years and the first one is done and dusted. There is hope for this candidate after all!

But there's more news yet, my darling Maasi, and it's more delicious than the paper.

Yes, I've done it again, against all my terrors and inhibitions. I've fallen in love. I had to just loosen up and relax and there it was staring me in the face, or rather, just across the hall. Yes, Maasi, it is Luke. Yeah, yeah, you told me so!

For six months now he has been working on me, the tricky man, gently, subtly worming his way into my heart – he knows I was rather fragile – just gently but firmly establishing his presence. For a red-blooded, serial-dating, true-blue American, the poor boy has been really very patient. And then, when he thought the time was ripe he made his move; he bloody recited Kalidas to me in Sanskrit, with translation accompanying!

Without going into detail, let us say things worked out rather well after an initial hiccup or two. Now don't you all start planning mehendis and sangeets and stuff like that. I am very happy, very quiet and sure of myself and so I think is Luke. We have something that appears very real and we're prepared to work at it and see where it leads us. I have my doctorate to finish and he will be winding up by end of semester and is likely to get a post-doc in Chicago, so it'll be a long-distance relationship for some time, at least till I complete the dissert. So just chill and wish me luck; at least I've jumped off the cliff and into the deep end, something I thought I'd never do again!

It's early morning here and I know you will see this mail before you get home and I simply had to write to you. I will Skype in a few hours – 8 p.m. your time – so that Mummy, Vishy uncle and you are all together. Don't tell them, just keep them together in the drawing room.

I keep remembering that Sufi quote you are so fond of:

'Whatever way Love's camels take,

that is my religion and my faith'

Well, love's camels have brought me to this present pass and I'll go where they take me. I'm no longer afraid.

Love you, Abha Maasi.

Akku

Epilogue

From: Abha Patel <abhaedits@abcmail.com>
To: Gayatri Bansal <gpbansal@mailer.com>

Dear ben,

Finally, a lighting of the lamps! The present Srimati Qureshi – God bless her grasping soul – has agreed to give my beloved Mo a divorce. Yes, she signed the papers and they have been filed on grounds of mutual incompatibility, long separation, and all this with mutual consent. A solid cash transfer was needed to grease the wheels, of course. Let's see how long the process takes. Fingers crossed, and he might still make an honest woman of me in my middle age! The silly witch didn't realize all these years that I'm too damn old to have children and that M loves his kids too much anyway to give the moolah to his doosari! Not that I fully understand the workings of her mind, of course.

It was delightful having Akku and her Luke over. He's a good man and God knows she deserves one. When are you and Vishy coming up? The weather's glorious and my tiny garden is ablaze with flowers. See you soon, I hope.

All my love,

Abha

Acknowledgements

THREE PEOPLE ARE PRIMARILY RESPONSIBLE FOR THIS novella appearing in its present form:

My wife Sandhya who did not approve of the first draft written years ago and insisted I rewrite the whole thing; my agent Preeti Gill who liked the final product and was confident that it would find a publisher; and my editor at Pan Macmillan India, Teesta Guha Sarkar, who accepted the manuscript and worked very hard at making it publication-worthy.

Thank you all, for everything.